Yardbird

Yardbird

A Scratch Williams Mystery

Mark Slade

Yardbird *yärd'bərd*, Noun (informal-US) 1 a convict, 2 one assigned to menial tasks legal, or illegal, performed for a powerful person or persons.

For Tracey, Zoey, Chachi, and of course, Betty Jane, who always loved a good mystery
And for William "Gatz" Hjortsberg for writing *Falling Angel*

"Damn, what's the world coming to?"
Dozen Grant

1

Old man Spiff snarled at Scratch Williams and spat in the fire. The flames rose from the mixture of gin and saliva. Scratch plucked at his glass eye uneasily, took out the black marble, and then put it back in. He couldn't figure out whether the damn thing was making him uncomfortable or Spiff was. Regardless, the hole where his left eye used to be was twitching something awful.

A piece of paper was at Scratch's feet. A memo addressed to Spiff and signed by his lawyer, Dan Lowery. Without bending down to pick it up, Scratch could make out only three words on the paper because of the badly lit room. Cherry Tree Hill.

"Mr Spiff," Scratch said, wringing his hands. "I took care of Gilmore and that bunch trying to unionize..."

"Ray Gardner!" Spiff screamed. "I don... I don't care about Gilmore and those... yo-yos in the union! I want Ray Gardner gone!"

"Mr Spiff, with all due respect, I'm a little sick of chasing your daughter's boyfriends out of town..."

"I don't give a shit what you do, yardbird," Spiff pointed a crooked finger at Scratch. "I want that son of a bitch out of my town."

"I haven't seen the man do anything wrong..."

"He fucked my daughter!"

Scratch cringed, not just at the word, but at the old man's use of it in terms of his own relation. He didn't like Spiff very much. He didn't like working for the Pinnacle board of trustees. He didn't much like yardbirdin' either, but it sure as hell beat working in the cotton fields – or oil fields, for that matter. Oliver Spiff owned Odarko just like he owned Reliance Oil. Reliance was one of six companies that set up shop in the Tri-county area of southwest Oklahoma.

"I think that's just gossip, Spiff," Scratch said.

The old man looked him up and down.

"Gossip can be gospel, yardbird," Spiff said. He limped away from the fireplace and sat in his oversized velvet chair. He poured himself another drink, Scotch this time. "I don't care what it is, from the mouth of babes to the pope, whores talkin' dirty, lies or truth. I want Ray Gardner out of my town dead or alive. Do what I pay you to do, yardbird."

Scratch made a face, and murmured: "Son of a bitch." He placed his hat on his head and sighed. "Yes sir."

"Gardner's staying at the Primrose," Spiff said. He watched Scratch pick up a yellow envelope from the end table. "There's three hundred bucks and a one-way ticket. Put him on a train to California."

"Three hundred bucks? You payin' him off?"

"I ain't payin' him off, you moron! That's six weeks' wages."

"Why not the bus? You usually throw 'em on the bus..."

"Don't worry about what I usually do! Just get this done, yardbird. And don't tell Shep about this."

That was odd. Shep Howard was Spiff's boy, and the sheriff of Odarko. Shep used to be the Yardbird for Spiff and Pinnacle back in the thirties. Doing all the dirty work for old rich assholes, everything from making oil rig boys behave to handling blackmail and spying on husbands and wives cheating on each other. Not for the faint-hearted.

That all changed when Shep caught the silver hammer killer. One of the oil rig boys went nutty and started slamming women in the head, tying up the bodies to beds with their own stockings and defiling them. Shep caught the guy in the act, shot him three times in the chest. The man died with his dick in his hands. The woman he was defiling didn't die from her wounds but she did wake up in time to see what he was doing. Katlin Grove hadn't been the same ever since. So Pinnacle made Shep Sheriff. He'd been at that post for 15 years. He was a trusted company man. Why wouldn't he want Shep to know about the usual deal of running Maggie Spiff's boyfriends out of town?

"OK, Spiff," Scratch said. "I won't say a word to Shep."

The old man looked sour. "You're damned right you won't." He drained his glass and smacked his lips. "Or I'll get a new yardbird to get rid of you."

2

Maggie Spiff stood at the top of the stairs looking like a statue of a Greek goddess, her arms folded around her abundant cleavage. Her tangled brown hair was up in a bun, one strand hanging down past her big brown eyes. She was in a green silk nightgown that clung to the ideal body that represented bombshell beauties of those days. Her mother's Italian features showed through in Maggie. It was a fact that Oliver Spiff had been traveling in Italy to make a deal with the powers that ran that boot land to bring his father's custom suits there. Spiff met Maggie's mother and practically shanghaied her to Texas.

She ran off more times the Texas Rangers or the OHP could count. Every time they'd catch up with Isabella, she was shacked up with somebody else. Which is how Maggie was born. As everyone suspected, Maggie's real father was half-black, half-Kichai Indian. Another fact, Oliver Spiff had the Texas Rangers kill Isabella's boyfriend.

Nine months later, Maggie was born.

Scratch looked up at her. They locked eyes. She smirked and let out a long sigh.

"You doin' my daddy's dirty work again?"

"I'm always doing you daddy's dirty work," Scratch said.

"Mmm." Maggie nodded. "Because of little old me, I suppose."

Scratch put his fedora on his balding head. "It's always about you, Miss Maggie."

She shrugged. "Can't get through this life without raisin' some hell."

"Ah. Yes. That might be true." Scratch laughed. "So, uh, Miss Maggie?"

"Yes, Mr Williams?"

"Just to let you know... that truck driver who made that record singin'?"

"What about him, Mr Williams?"

"I saw him on Ed Sullivan."

"Is that a fact, Mr Williams?"

"That's a fact, Miss Spiff," Scratch said. He headed to the front door of Spiff Manor. He twisted the door knob and turned to Maggie. "He took that beating I gave him like a real man. Looks like his face healed real good."

"I'm glad, Mr Williams," was all she said. No conscience about getting that man into trouble or in danger of death. Just cold like. Real damn cold.

"You should've held on to him, ma'am. Yep. That boy has talent," Scratch crossed the threshold and called out: "I think he's going to make a lot of money."

3

Scratch pulled up in front of the Primrose hotel in his '48 Dodge. The building was one of the tallest in Odarko, other than the Reliance offices. The Primrose was run by an old Jewish fella from Budapest. Jerzy Gerkbahn. Scratch was the only one who knew Jerzy's real heritage. If people in Odarko knew, the Klan would hang his ass by Moonbark Tree in the park just to show everyone they didn't allow his kind to run things in town. Actually, it would have been a message to Darktown. Stay in your place.

Jerzy had hired Scratch to find his brother, Konny. He disappeared just after they came to Oklahoma with their mother. She was the one who bought the building and turned it into a hotel in 1938. Konny liked to drink, raise a little hell. Scratch traced the man's last days. Apparently, he was robbed out in Darktown. An eyewitness to the account was Frito Barnes, who owned an illegal gin joint back in those days. Konny liked his women dark, dangerous, and more than willing to do things in public.

Out back, behind Barnes's gin joint, three men came up behind Konny and cut him to ribbons while he was having sex with one of the local prostitutes. Barnes came out to throw away trash and saw the whole thing. They rolled him in an old pickup, and drove toward Pleasant Lake. Nothing pleasant about that body of water. People picnic out there in the day. At night, it was a dumping ground for the dead.

The info he gave to Jerzy netted Scratch a few hundred. Neither man let old Spiff know of the outside job. Spiff would have run Scratch out of Odarko. He was possessive like that. Evidence shows. Look what Scratch had to do at the moment. Scratch had long ago come to the conclusion the old man was nuts.

Scratch finished his cigarette and tossed it in a mud puddle on the street. He got out of the Dodge, slow and deliberate like his walk. He stepped up to the drugstore and stood at the door. Scratch checked his wristwatch. Six thirty-five. Harry Sanders would lock the doors soon. The door swung open fast, and a bell chimed.

Harry popped up from behind the counter. His face, with its fleshy jowls, was flushed. No doubt the little fat druggist was putting away a new batch of pornographic photos and magazines. He caught his breath and chuckled. He came from behind the counter.

"Oh," Harry said, "it's only you, Scratch. How's tricks?"

"Expecting somebody else, Harry?" Scratch asked.

"No, no." Harry threw his hands up. "Just pleased to see you." He ran a finger over his pencil-thin mustache. "Can I get you an ice-cream soda?"

Scratch shook his head. "Not tonight, Harry. I need to use your phone, if that's all right?"

"Of course." Harry flipped a nickel to Scratch.

Scratch barely caught it. "And that's why you will never pitch for the Yankees."

Harry swatted the air. "Ah, who wants to play for those pansies?"

"For the right money…" Scratch let his words trail off. Harry just shook his head, walked away muttering something about the Kansas Athletics winning the World Series one day.

Scratch put the nickel in the slot and he heard a smooth female voice on the line.

"What can I do for you?" The operator asked.

Scratch smiled sheepishly. He leaned in to the pay phone, hung his head.

"You could have dinner with me," Scratch said.

The operator clucked her tongue. "Sir, I'm only a telephone operator. I'm providing a service."

"I'm sorry," Scratch chuckled. "Your voice sends me over the moon."

Scratch couldn't help himself. The woman reminded him of a school teacher he had in the eighth grade, Scratch's last year. They shared that same commanding, smooth-as-velvet voice, telling you what to do in a precise, well-mannered way. Mrs Donner was her name. She was a solid woman, but not overweight, just tall and shapely. Her honey-brown hair was always fashioned neatly in a bun and her thinly framed glasses always sat at end of her nose. She always wore a white blouse and a black skirt, and black open-toed heels. You couldn't find a wrinkle or a crease in her clothes. When she walked, her stockings rubbed together, creating a rhythm like a whispering ticking clock.

He often wondered what happened to Mrs Donner. Maybe she married a wealthy businessman and had a couple of kids. Or she ended up running a clothing shop in Tulsa. Or she tutored kids for her regular income. Maybe she spent her nights alone thinking about all the students she taught.

Scratch hoped she'd think of him once in a while.

Scratch used to imagine all kinds of things he'd do with Mrs Donner. Now he imagines all those things he'd like to do with the telephone operator. He wondered if she was a blonde or a redhead. Maybe the same hair color as Mrs Donner.

The operator wasn't pleased at all with that confession. She sounded incensed. "Another one."

"Another?" Scratch said. "What do you mean by that?"

The operator let out an angry sigh. "I mean just that. Another one! A nutcase! Look, you want a number or what?"

"Yeah, yeah. I'm in a hurry anyway, but we'll continue this..."

"The number! Give it to me!" The operator said.

Scratch smiled. Yeah, he thought. I think I'm in love.

"Waltzing 224."

"Thank you," she said in that smooth, commanding voice and Scratch drew in a sharp breath, released it slowly. "Connecting."

The line buzzed. A soft male voice answered in an Eastern-European accent.

"Primrose Hotel."

"Jerzy, old pal," Scratch crooned. "How's it hangin'?"

"I'm sorry? Can I help you sir?" Jerzy asked.

"It's Scratch, Jerzy."

"Mr Williams," he sighed. "Oh my. Been a few months since I've spoken to you. You didn't come dinner as my wife requested."

"Yeah, sorry about that. Been busy," Scratch said.

"Of course," Jerzy said. "I explained to Clara you were almost always on call. No matter, I am forever indebted to you for the job you performed."

"It was nothing, Jerzy," Scratch said. "Say, uh... could you do me a favor?"

"Well, of course!" Jerzy exclaimed, his voice pitched a little higher with each syllable. "Jerzy Gerkbahn takes care of his friends – always!"

Scratch chuckled. "I know, Jerzy, I know. Anyway, uh, look," he licked his lips as he came up with a suitable lie. "Say... a friend of mine has a room at your establishment."

"Is that so?"

"Yeah... uh... Jerzy. His name is Gardner. Ray Gardner."

"Oh, yes." Jerzy sniffed. "I know Mr Gardner."

"We're supposed to have a party at my place." Scratch stopped to make sure Jerzy was listening.

After a brief pause, Jerzy said: "Ah. Yes."

"Thing is, old pal." Scratch chuckled. "I can't have it at my place. My mother is in town..."

"Oh! How wonderful! Give her my love!"

"Yeah, yeah, sure. That's the reason we can't have our party," Scratch said, squinting with concentration as he made the story up on the spot.

"Uh-huh." Jerzy sounded slightly confused. "Does she not like parties because of the noise?"

Scratch laughed. "Let's just say... she wouldn't like what went on at these parties."

"Oh?" Jerzy still didn't understand what Scratch was getting at.

"Yeah, old pal. I'd bring the booze and Ray would bring the ladies."

Jerzy laughed. "Oh. Yes. Yes, of course. I see. Well, it seems Mr Gardner has already started without you in his room."

"Is that right?" Scratch said, very interested. "You know…" Scratch chuckled. "I forgot what room number he said he'd be in."

"Oh… uh…" Jerzy pulled away from the phone, his voice on the line reflected that. He bounced back, his voice louder and sharper. "Room number one-o-three."

"Thanks, pal," Scratch said.

"Mmm. He has a young lady already in there. As a matter of fact, I've had one or two complaints about the loud music. Frankly – please forgive me, Mr Williams – I don't like your friend very much."

"That's OK, Jerzy," Scratch said. "Not many people do. Say. The favor?"

"Oh," Jerzy cleared his throat. "Yes? What would it be?"

"Well, it's a silly game Ray and I play. We like to – uh – scare each other. Practical jokes and all."

"Oh. All right. Is this an American folly?"

"Uh, yeah. Sure. Could you leave me the pass key?"

Total silence. Damn, Scratch thought. Maybe I went too far with that last part. After a few seconds, Jerzy spoke.

"Yes," he said in a quiet voice. "When you come in the hotel, give me a wave. I will hand you the evening paper. The key will be inside."

Jerzy hung up quickly, leaving a couple of clicking noises in Scratch's ears. He waited for the operator.

"Hang up now, please," she demanded.

Scratch smiled. "That's all I wanted, baby, was to hear you say that."

"Weirdo!" The operator said in a huff.

The line went dead and Scratch placed the receiver on the cradle. When Scratch turned around, Harry was standing behind him, scowling.

"What's wrong?" Scratch asked.

"Nothing," Harry said. He was stony-faced, ice in his voice. He handed Scratch an envelope.

"What's this?"

"For the old man," Harry said, glaring at Scratch.

Scratch looked inside. There was 100 dollars in 10s and 20s. Scratch didn't understand.

"No," Scratch said. "What's this for?"

"When you see Gardner," Harry snarled. "You ask him what it's for. Now get out, will ya? I'm closing up."

Scratch nodded. "Yeah. All right." He shuffled out the door, tipped his hat to Harry.

"And tell the old man and your friend they can both hang!" Harry slammed the door, locked it and pulled the blinds.

Scratch sat in his car for a few minutes.

"What was all that about?" he asked himself, turning the envelope over in his hands.

A red Plymouth Fury sped by, blaring *Train kept a-rollin'* by Johnny Burnette Rock 'n Roll Trio. A fair-haired boy with small black eyes and a crooked smile gawked at Scratch the whole time he drove by. The boy had a small round head with a flat top so large the air force could land a jet plane on it. In the passenger seat Scratch could see a brown-haired girl cuddling up to the boy. For a second, Scratch thought it was Maggie Spiff.

He felt uneasy about it when he thought back. No more than 45 minutes ago he'd left her at the top of the stairs ready for bed. The old man had the house pretty much locked up. He had his security patrolling the property. So it couldn't have been her anyway.

All Scratch knew was that boy gave him the shivers.

4

The Primrose was the nicest building in Odarko. By nicest, it was always clean, very elegant. A lot of Texas businessmen used the Primrose as a stayover from too many parties, to rest up, or just as a cover story for their wives when they were really at the California Club whoring and boozing. The Primrose had three floors and 110 rooms. All with the same burgundy carpet the lobby had.

There were 110 rooms. Why it stopped on that number is God's little secret. Inside, each had two small doubles or one queen size. A liquor cabinet, a kitchenette, and a bathroom where the queen of England herself would be proud to powder her nose. They had bellhops and room service that didn't close until 1am. Wallpaper from Paris, France, depicting the plight of Joan of Arc, and chandeliers from Florence, Italy. Not many townspeople could afford a room at the Primrose.

That's why it befuddled Scratch that an oil worker could afford to stay in a place like that. A wage of 50 dollars a week didn't stretch to such accommodations. Usually the men that worked for Reliance stayed at the Courtyard, which was a trailer park. Or Joan Hoss's Room and Board, which most didn't, because Miss Hoss didn't allow beer or booze in her house. Or maybe, if they were lucky, renting a house on the edge of Darktown from Peter Dodd, the local slumlord.

Sure enough, Jerzy left the pass key in the evening paper lying on the sign-in desk. When Scratch entered the lobby, he gave Jerzy a wave. He walked to the desk and Jerzy pointed to the paper.

Scratch placed the paper under his arms, started to walk away and stopped. He leaned on the desk with both elbows.

"Uh, is there any mail for me?" Scratch asked, looked around the nearly empty lobby.

"I'll check for you, sir," Jerzy said. He was amused with the charade he and Scratch were carrying in front of practically no one and really, no one cared. Jerzy pretended to look in cubby holes, pulling envelopes and stationary paper out, placing them back.

One big-shot oil man sat in a velvet chair looking at a copy of Life magazine with a girl in her pajamas on the cover. He looked up from the magazine. The fat man wrinkled his nose at Scratch, exhaled a heavy sigh. Scratch smiled back. The oil man shifted uneasily in his chair and flipped the pages of the magazine like he was angry at the world.

"No sir," Jerzy said. "I'm afraid not."

A very attractive, overdressed young woman stepped out of the elevator, her heels tapping away as she sashayed across the floor of the lobby.

The oil man jumped from the velvet chair and trotted to her. His tiny, spindly legs almost gave out under him. Scratch watched the scene unfold. The oil man couldn't keep his fat, stubby hands off the blonde, and she only let him give her a peck on the cheek. He nervously walked her out of the Primrose's door.

The oil man opened the door of a Chevrolet Bel Air and ushered her in. The woman got in indifferently, making sure her skirt was out of the way when the oil man shut the door. A long, salacious grin was on the man's face. He clapped his hands and shook out a spark of energy from his body. He ran around to the other side, happy as a child on Christmas day.

"You can't believe your luck, huh, pal?" Scratch said.

"I'm sorry sir?" Jerzy said.

Scratch shook his head. "Nothing," he tipped his hat. "Nothing at all," he said, moving toward the elevator.

Inside the elevator, he checked the paper for the pass key. He unrolled the paper and the skeleton key fell to the floor of the elevator with a loud clank. Scratch dropped to his knees and retrieved it. The elevator door opened and a woman appeared. She started to enter but saw Scratch crouched at her legs. She gave out a muted shriek, backed away.

Scratch immediately stood. He tipped his hat to the stunned woman. "Sorry, ma'am." He brushed by her.

Scratch looked for the room. The numbers seemed to be flipped. The lower numbers were at the end of the hallway and on the wrong side. In the hotels Scratch had stayed in on his leave in the Army after boot camp and when he was released, the even numbers were on the right, odd numbers on the left. At the Primrose, it was switched.

All he really had to do was follow the loud, muffled music. There it was. Room 103. Two rooms from the fire escape. Half-way down the hall, Scratch heard two female voices singing *Tonight, you belong to me.* Scratch stood at the door and listened. He heard a man's voice, a female's voice, and both of them laughing.

Scratch eased the skeleton key into the lock. He pulled the door knob to him and turned the right. The lock popped. Quietly, he rolled the knob and the door opened. Scratch waited, listened. He heard a wet sound, loud slurping. The door creaked as it swung open.

Scratch stepped inside the room, but kept the door open.

A young blonde woman in her late teens was on her knees, her face buried in Gardner's unbuttoned fly, her mouth wrapped around his bent penis. Her pony tail swung as her head bobbed up and down. Gardner's eyes were closed, his back arched. His hips swiveled slightly as he moaned. The young woman's eyes darted toward Scratch and pulled away from Gardner's crotch.

The young woman screamed. She retreated, using her hands and feet to crawl backwards. She fell on her back, and felt for her high heels. In one swoop she grabbed them, got to her feet and zipped past Scratch, breathing hard. Scratch laughed, noticing her stockings had slipped down her legs.

Gardner uttered a few obscenities and some harsh words at the young woman, but she was already down the hallway. She jumped inside the lift as soon as the doors opened. Gardner struggled to put away his erect penis. He pulled his trousers up and buttoned them quickly. He balled his fists up. His face, already flushed, turned bright red. His lips and nose contorted as he spluttered nonsense at Scratch.

The song on the radio ended. A DJ came on, announced that song was by Patience and Prudence. After that, a barrage of commercials assaulted everyone in the hotel room and the hallway.

"Who the hell are you?" Gardner screamed.

"You know me," Scratch said. His calm demeanor seemed to anger Gardner even more.

"I don't know you..." He stopped, eyed Scratch. He nodded. "Yeah," he said in a sour tone. "I know you, buddy." Gardner walked to the nightstand, grabbed the bottle of Gold's whiskey. He poured some in a long glass more than likely stolen from a bar. "You're the old man's yardbird."

Scratch smiled, tipped his hat. "What're you gonna do? Have to make a living somehow."

"By spying on the working class for the rich?" Gardner took a sip. He stopped drinking and pointed to the door. "Hey! You mind shuttin' the damn door!" He gulped down the rest of the whiskey, sat the glass down on the nightstand and poured more. This time he filled the long glass halfway.

"That glass looks familiar," Scratch said. "You get that at Fleming's bar?"

Gardner drained the glass and smacked his lips. He shrugged. "So what? What's it matter to you, huh? You a bar detective tracking down every glass and bottle of booze stolen?"

"Hmm! That ain't a bad idea, Ray," Scratch said.

"So what the hell do you want, yardbird?"

Scratch removed an envelope from the inside pocket of his jacket, tossed it on the bed. "Spiff wants you gone."

"Does he now?" Gardner laughed. "He's a miserable old bastard because he takes it up the ass."

Scratch nodded. "I'll agree with that. Still, the old man wants you out of Odarko and Oklahoma. There's 300 dollars and a train ticket to California. I suggest you take it and dangle."

Gardner glared at Scratch.

"Look, fella." Scratch moved toward Gardner slowly, with caution. "The old man wants you to disappear, one way... or another."

"What? You going to kill me?" Gardner laughed. "You really don't know who I am. Do you?"

"I don't care," Scratch said. "Spiff didn't like the fact you... had relations with his daughter."

"Daughter?" Gardner thought about it. "I never met the old man's daughter."

"Enough talking!" Scratch raised his voice. The little cat and mouse play was getting him hot under the collar.

"You're the one doing the talkin', Captain," Gardner said. "I think it's time you started walkin'."

The commercials ended on the radio. The DJ announced the next song was *Allegheny Moon* by Patti Page.

He saw Garner's hand slip in the drawer of the nightstand, and the butt of a snub nose .38 began to appear. Scratch charged Gardner and took hold of the hand bringing out the gun. The fedora slipped off Scratch's head sailed to the bed. They struggled for 30 seconds before Gardner brought his knee into Scratch's crotch. Scratch yelped and dropped to the floor just as Gardner brought down the barrel of the .38 on top of his head.

Scratch fell sideways. He tried to shake off the consummate pain surging in his forehead and eyes. He saw Gardner's boot coming towards his face. Scratch caught the man's left leg and tipped him over. Now Gardner was on the floor next to Scratch. Gardner felt three swift punches to the kidney. He cried out, tried to roll away, but Scratch had a hold of his collar with one hand, and drove his fist into the bridge of Gardner's nose. Something popped. Blood flowed from a mess of broken cartilage and bruised flesh.

Scratch got to his feet. He found a suitcase under the bed and tossed it on the mattress.

"You're leaving town, Gardner," Scratch said, unlatched the suitcase and started gathering clothes from the mahogany dresser where the radio sat. "Either by bus or by coffin. You're leaving Odarko for good."

He opened a drawer on the bottom and found clothing that shouldn't belong to Ray Gardner. Different colors, styles of panties. Stockings, garter belts, bras. Scratch was a little confused at first. Did he wear these? Then he saw names on torn pieces of paper attached to the undergarments. Suzie, Debbie, Flora. That made more sense. He was collecting the things of women he'd been with. Scratch laughed.

He showed Gardner a pair of woolen stockings with the name Clara written on a piece of paper attached to them.

"These don't belong old Mrs Grace, do they?" Scratch said. "You like grandmas, too?"

Gardner laid on the floor, cupping his bleeding nose in his hands, sobbing. He was wailing, as if he was in terrible pain, and muttering he was going to kill Scratch. He saw Scratch reach for a black hatbox sitting on top of the dresser. What caught Scratch's eye was the gold initials SS, gleaming in the lights.

"Gardner, You naughty boy," Scratch laughed. "You collecting women's hats, too?"

Scratch moved the hatbox slightly and saw a medium-sized hole had been made in the wall. He bent down to peer through it, but scuffing sounds from the floor caught his attention.

"Don't touch that!" Gardner's voice was muffled by the hand still trying to keep blood from getting on his shirt, which in fact was something he was doing a piss-poor job at.

Scratch looked at him incredulously. He scoffed, reached for the black hatbox with gold string. He heard two sets of heeled shoes behind him. He heard a metallic sound. Possibly the hammer of a gun clicking. Scratch wasn't sure. He turned to see.

That's when everything went black.

5

The darkness remained, but a muffled voice screamed at him. The voice spoke Korean and Scratch only knew three phrases in that language. What the voice said, he couldn't understand. And when Scratch didn't answer a hard slap or punch in the kidneys would occur. The torture worsened.

Water dripped on his face for an hour before the voice returned, screaming at him. Again, Scratch didn't understand what was said. A punch in the kidney, and the wooden chair he was bound to was tipped over. A kick in the face came next. He felt the presence of someone else. He smelled their breath, felt them breathing. They didn't say a word for several minutes.

Scratch and the chair were returned to normal position. He heard boots descend, echoing on a wooden floor. He heard a door open and shut, then lock. Nothing happened for three hours.

* * *

Scratch couldn't take it anymore.

Living in Darktown, no job, no job prospects. Just sitting on Dobro's front porch, drinking swill from a jar and cuttin' up. So Scratch joined the Army. Dobro begged him not to go. Fighting in a white man's war. Had nothing to do with him or his family, killing Chinese people.

What else was there to do in Darktown? He wasn't allowed in Odarko, like other black folk. If anyone from Darktown ventured into the main town, they got harassment in the daytime, lynching at night. So they set up their own businesses, greengrocer, owned by Leon, produce stable, owned by Leon's brother Homer, and the three lookouts where you could get a proper drink – the Owl, the Redpiper and the Frolic – were co-owned by the Morrison brothers.

Even Scratch's sister Imelda told him not to leave Darktown.

"There's nothing outside of Darktown for you, Scratch," Immy said.

"Ain't nothing inside Darktown for me, either," Scratch told her.

Immy snorted. "Just because you look white don't mean they ain't gonna find out where you from."

Scratch shrugged. "You could look white."

"Not like you, Scratch," Immy said.

Their father was Paul Gruber, a German who came to America for a better life after World War One and ended up as a bootlegger in Odarko. He took a shine to a golden-skinned young woman by the name of Sherry Williams. She'd been married at 14 to the Morrison brothers' cousin, Carter. That marriage produced no children and lasted until she was 18. Technically, she and Carter never dissolved their relationship by law. But she also never took Carter's last name.

She took up with Gruber but he never lived with her. For good reason. Gruber already had a wife and two boys and a girl. Sherry became pregnant with Allan. Then Imelda, a year later. Gruber kept up house with both women. They each knew about the other, but never met. Danika and her children lived in Cottonwood County, 20 miles from Odarko. Danika struggled with money and food just like Sherry did because, in spite of all the money Paul Gruber made, he spent most of it gambling, whoring or drinking.

Paul Gruber was stabbed to death in a Tulsa nightclub over 10 dollars owed to a man no one could identify and the police had no interest in catching. At least, that;s what everyone was told.

At 12 and 11, Allan and Imelda went to live with Danika's sister Collen in Tulsa while Sherry worked in all three lookouts, serving drinks or hosting live shows. That's where they got most of their education and the lie that both of them were of Spanish descent. Allan hated it in Tulsa. He was the first to leave, aged 14. Imelda stayed until she was 16. She flourished in school, even had a scholarship to Oklahoma State.

Sherry died just as Immy was ready to go to college.

Immy didn't take the scholarship. They both ended up back in Darktown, living in the shack Gruber bought for their mother.

Stealing produce from his uncle and selling it in Horace County got Scratch and Dobro in trouble. Uncle Homer's men got wind of it one night. They chased Dobro's old pickup down highway 20 and started shooting at them. Dobro lost control, the pickup slammed in a tree. Uncle Homer's men thought they were dead, so kept on driving.

Funny enough, Dobro didn't get hurt at all. No broken bones. Not a mark on his body. Scratch, well, he lost his right eye. Had to use a marble for a while until Uncle Homer took him to Tulsa, saw a doctor and bought him a glass eye. Uncle Homer wasn't as cold-blooded as people thought. He just didn't like his own blood to steal from him.

To everyone's amazement, the army took Scratch. The doctor didn't even examine the men sent to him. He just signed everyone's papers and sent them to boot camp. The sergeant questioned Scratch about getting past the doctor and Scratch didn't have an answer. After that, no one else even mentioned his eye or how he got in the army. Nearly a year went by when Joe Turner, who was in boot camp with Scratch, had the answer. Turned out the doctor went home and shot himself. By that time, Scratch was in Korea, defending the name of a mountain he couldn't pronounce.

* * *

The darkness didn't succumb to light for a long time. The torture continued, but there were long bouts of silence from his torturers. They kept asking him questions in a language he didn't understand. Scratch never talked. He did scream a lot and begged them to stop.

One day, light came. So did explosions and gunfire. People screamed. He heard the voices of women and children call out to their God as death came for them. Scratch heard American voices. There was a familiar smell of tainted clothing and the grease used to clean guns.

A hand pulled the scarf from Scratch's eyes. A square-jawed man with thin lips and tiny black eyes was facing him. He was a private, just like Scratch. Tommy Dilleo was his name, as Scratch later learned. They stared at each other for a few seconds.

Scratch looked past him to see about 20 American GIs standing in a hut, with what looked to be a family. Four women of varying ages, three little boys and one little girl. There was also an old man who might have been the grandfather and most likely Scratch's torturer. The awful smell Scratch kept smelling was boiled cabbage. A GI stirred the pot on a wood stove, raked green and white leaves with a spoon. He showed it to his buddy, who made a face.

"Anybody want some kimchi?" The GI bellowed. No takers. Some laughed, some cried out in disgust.

Tommy untied Scratch from the chair.

Tears rolled down Scratch's cheeks.

"Hey, bud, stay where you are, OK? Everything's fine. The cavalry is here," Tommy called out. He stopped Scratch from standing. "Can we get a medic over here?" He smiled at Scratch, patted him lightly on the shoulder. "Ah, hell, soldier. You'll be OK!"

"I don't even know what happened..." Scratch said as his chest heaved. He tried to control the sobbing but he was too overwhelmed with conflicted emotions. The medic came over and started to work on Scratch.

"Hey fellas, this guy must be Superman or somethin'! Look it! He went through all this crap and never spilled where we were!"

Scratch laughed.

"What's so funny?" Tommy asked.

"I couldn't tell 'em," Scratch said.

Tommy looked at Scratch sideways. "Why is that?"

"I couldn't understand a damn thing he was saying."

6

Scratch awoke in the '48 Dodge to the smooth sounds of Sinatra crooning *In the Wee Small Hours of the Morning*. And it was just that. The wee hours of the morning. The sun was just coming up and the sky was pink and grey. The birds were singing not a song of hope for the new day, but a warning or caution of something atrocious.

He realized he was in the driver's side of the car.

When he opened his eyes, he still had a blurry vision of an old Korean man screaming at him. Scratch immediately felt for an imaginary gun in the breast pocket of his coat. The mist cleared from his eyes and a teenaged girl started shrieking. She turned and ran into the arms of a teenaged boy. Suddenly, Scratch was surrounded by people in the cul-de-sac where the Dodge was parked.

Scratch looked to his right and saw a dead man slumped over in the passenger side. He pulled the body up to face him. Just as he thought. It was Ray Gardner. He heard sirens behind him. Scratch adjusted the rearview mirror and saw the two police cars and an ambulance clearly marked Coleman County. Scratch sighed.

Someone drove me and my dead friend 35 miles from Odarko, he thought. Why didn't they just dump us both at Kemora Lake? It was only five miles away. Then again, they'd have to drive through Darktown to get there.

Scratch's face ached. His right eye itched him. He moved the rearview mirror so he could look at his face. His glass eye was gone, leaving his right eye a huge black hole.

He started to remember what happened.

He reached for the hatbox and somebody hit him. Just before he passed out, he had heard two sets of heels on the floor and the door slamming shut. Whoever hit Scratch from behind took his glass eye when it came out. He looked over at Gardner and saw a bullet hole in his forehead. In Gardner's lap was the snub-nose .38 he had pulled on Scratch.

"Son of a bitch," Scratch said.

Scratch felt the barrel of a .357 Magnum touch his cheek.

"Don't move, peckerwood!" he heard Deputy Marian Shaw call out.

Scratch moved his eyes and saw Sheriff Rooster Magee standing tall in the horizontal and bloated in the vertical. He was leaning on the open door of his '52 Ford. The radio was blaring George Jones singing *Run, Boy, Run*. A huge ball of chaw sat in Rooster's left cheek until he decided to switch it to his right, hock some of it in the back of his throat and splatter the blacktop with it. He walked toward the Dodge.

Shaw grabbed Scratch by his coat, pulled him out the car window and tossed him on the highway. He kicked Scratch in the stomach. Scratch coughed, doubled up and wrapped his arms around his midsection. Shaw holstered his weapon and laughed.

"I told you not to move, buckcherry! Didn't I Sheriff?"

"You most certainly did, Deputy Shaw," Rooster leaned down and said to Scratch: "You in a lot of trouble, boy."

* * *

"Deputy Shaw," Rooster said. "I wish you would reconsider your leaving law enforcement, especially Coleman County. But I understand how you and your wife have struggled, and your desire to head to California. I wish you luck, son."

Rooster perfected his version of the John Wayne walk when he used to be a rodeo cowboy. His claim was that he invented that walk one night after lassoing three calves and ambling over to untie them. He put a little shake in his hips and four girls, two spic girls, one blonde and an Irish redhead seated in the front of the bleachers, whooped and hollered for him.

"Now." Rooster retold this story as he sat on the edge of his desk. Scratch was in the cell, lying on his bunk, his fedora covering his face, trying not to listen to Rooster. "You wouldn't believe it, but that walk has gotten me laid more times than I can count. I bedded all four of those young lassies. Still got up and baled hay for old man Spiff out in Cottonwood. Before he built Odarko into what it is today. Of course," he shrugged. "I'm talking about George Spiff. The father of that rat turd Oliver Spiff. Your boss, I believe?"

Shaw laughed along with Rooster. "I love that story, Sheriff," he confessed, love in his bulging eyes.

Rooster looked at Shaw sideways. "Of course you do! Because it's the truth, son."

Scratch shook his head. Made a loud clucking noise with his tongue.

"You got somethin' to say?" Shaw screamed, touching the butt of his .357 in its holster. Rooster waved him back and Shaw eased back in the wooden chair.

"An out-of-work actor in the thirties got drunk in San Pedro, California, where I cut my teeth as a law officer," Rooster said, chugged coffee from a mug, wiped his thick lips. He saw this walk and took it with him to Hollywood. And that actor was Paul Fix." Rooster spat a black wad in the trash can. "The rest," Rooster said with a weird leering grin on his long, fat face, "is history. Hell, the closest those fags out there ever got to a real cowboy was when they bumper-car an asshole in the men's restroom. So how in blazes could they know such a manly walk?" He laughed. "Obviously from me!"

"Obviously!" Shaw mimicked Rooster.

Rooster cut his eyes at the young man. Shaw hung his head.

The door swung open and Shep Howard and his deputy, Ralph Far-ley, stepped through the jailhouse. Rooster and Shep locked eyes.

"Turn him loose," Shep said.

"Shep," Rooster said in a calm, and gentle way, like he was explaining a Bible story to children. "You don't walk into a man's jailhouse, let alone his county, and demand that man set free his A1 suspect."

"When you work for Oliver Spiff, you bound to do a lot of things you normally wouldn't do," Shep said. "Like gun down the sheriff of Coleman County and blow the balls off his deputy."

Rooster laughed. "They are hollow words, Shep. No meaning behind them a-tall. How many men have you really killed? Now," Rooster showed the butt of his Colt revolver to Shep. "I got 12 notches on this gun. Count 'em. Every one of 'em has a story, my friend."

"With not a shred of truth to them, Rooster and you damn well know it." Shep walked past Rooster and Shaw, who was in his gunfighter stance about as scary as Jerry Lewis screwing a football, and went into the office. Ralph went to the jail cell, spoke to Scratch.

"You all right?"

"About as all right as I can be," Scratch said.

"You had breakfast?" He asked.

"Just hot water with grounds in it."

Ralph patted the bars on the cell. "We'll go to Chauncey's on 61 when we get you out," he walked to the office, following Rooster inside.

"He ain't getting' out!" Shaw called out to Ralph. Ralph laughed. Shaw trotted over to the jail cell. "You ain't getting' out, peckerwood. You're so smug. Didn't even ask for a phone call or a lawyer... You ain't getting' out."

"You a bettin' man, Shaw?" Scratch asked.

Shaw thought about the question. "No," he said.

"Good," Scratch nodded. "You'd lose."

"I know who you really are," Shaw's upper lip curled. "I know what you came from."

"Is that a fact?"

"You know damn well it is, boy," Shaw said. "I've seen you in Darktown," he chewed on his bottom lip, scrunched up his eyes, trying to look intimidating. "I know what you really are. When I get a chance, I'm gonna let everybody in Odarko know. How's them beans now, peckerwood?"

"Taste like horseshit to me," Scratch said. "You don't know shit from Shinola. All you know is rumor and housewife talk. You a backdoor man, Shaw? You sleepin' in another man's bed after he done wrinkled the sheets? Huh?"

"Shut your dirty mouth. You need to find a church, peckerwood. Ask God for forgiveness, talking the way you do to a real white man."

Stone faced, Scratch scowled at Shaw.

"Hell do you mean by that?"

"Ohh-ho-ho! I think I finally got through to you," Shaw grinned, then added in a sing-song voice: "Like I said," he giggled. "I seened you in niggertown..."

Scratch leered at Shaw, shrugged. "So what? Maybe I was buying me some brown meat."

"Yeah? That would be against the law." Shaw sniffed, examining his fingernails. "You know, brother and sister... knowin' each other... carnally..?" He moved his eyes up slowly to meet Scratch's hard stare. "I think old man Spiff would be very upset if he knew that you awful close-knit, with some of the... *cuh-lard* folk. I mean, especially him bein' an honorary Grand Dragon of the Klan." Shaw licked his lips. "Whew-we! That cocoa-butter-colored girl you visit must be some piece! She could almost pass for a spic girl!"

Shaw guffawed and Scratch reached out to get him, but Shaw danced away from him, squealing, laughing harder.

"Shaw!" Rooster bellowed from doorway of his office. Shep and Ralph stood at arm's length from Rooster, both watching the scene unfold, both touching the butts of Smith and Wesson .38s, ready for anything going down. "Stop teasing that man and let him out of the cell!"

Shaw stopped dancing. The smile disappeared from his pale, flakey face. He looked at Rooster curiously.

"Go on!" Rooster demanded. "Git on with it! Turn Mr Williams loose!"

Shaw, resigned, head bowed almost to his chest, got the keys from a beat-up gun rack and picked one out. The door to the cell popped open as soon his wrists turned the key. Shep relaxed, took his hand off his gun. Ralph smiled, breathed a sigh of relief and did the same.

Shaw pulled on the bars and the cell door creaked open. Scratch stood, grabbed his coat, then his fedora. He smiled at Shaw and slowly placed his hat on his balding head. He walked past Shaw and said: "I'll be seeing you."

Indignant, nostrils flared, Shaw said: "You can count on it, pecker-wood!"

7

They were riding down the highway in Shep's Police car. Scratch was in the back, Shep was in the passenger seat, and Ralph was driving.

"The old man wants to see you," Shep said.

"I'm sure he does," Scratch said. His head was pounding and he felt like invisible pins were forcing his eyelids shut. He lay in the backseat, one arm covering his eyes to block out the sun.

"Somehow this misfortune ended up in the Daily Message," Ralph said.

"I thought the old man controlled the news," Scratch said.

"He did," Shep turned the radio on. He turned the knob through dead air and white noise until he came up on Johnny Cash singing *Train of Love*. He started tapping his finger on the car seat, keeping time with the brushes on the drums. "He never really owned the newspaper. That was Horace Hammock. Old Horace ain't with us no more."

"What happened to him?" Scratch asked. He remembered two years before, he'd taken care of a problem for Horace. A blackmail from an ex-reporter who went on a vacation with Horace. Seemed Horace ran a paper on the East coast, and had taken some money he shouldn't have. Invested that in a chocolate bar company. The blackmail stopped after one visit, and the reporter had relocated to Chicago where he accidently overdosed on heroin.

"Apparently..." Shep hocked up phlegm from deep down his throat and spat it out the window. "Horace killed himself."

"He didn't seem like the suicidal type," Scratch said.

"The old man didn't think so either," Ralph added.

"He wants me to look into it?" Scratch sat up in the back seat. "He'll have to look into it himself. I'm busy trying to figure out who set me up."

"You know you'll end up doing it," Shep said. "I know first hand, Scratch. You can't defy the old man."

"I'm different from you, Shep."

"I know." Shep's voice raised up a few decibels "I know, Scratch. But I used to be the yardbird in these parts. I'm just..."

"I'm different from you," Scratch said.

Shep chuckled. "OK," he said, throwing his hands up. "You're different. I guarantee you'll be doing what the old man wants. Priority is Horace and who put in that news story of Gardner's death."

"Shep?"

"Yeah?"

"Would the old man set me up?"

"What the hell for? You work for him."

Scratch shrugged. "I don't know. Maybe to keep me in line? A way out of something else?"

"Scratch, he don't operate that way," Shep said. "Now, if you left the company for any reason... and you made threats... or if he didn't trust you anymore..."

"Any reason he shouldn't trust you?" Ralph glanced at Scratch in the rearview mirror. "Or we shouldn't?"

"That's a hell of a question, Ralph!" Shep yelled.

"I'm sorry, Scratch. I had to ask,." Ralph said.

There was a moment of uneasy silence. Scratch's mind had drifted back to the incident at the Primrose. How he reached for that hatbox, how upset Gardner got, and suddenly he was out cold.

"Shep. I need to get back in that room at the Primrose," Scratch said.

"Well... I guess you can. The city boys are in there. County took the body already. In a few hours Gladys and her girls will start cleaning up blood and brain."

"What about my car, Shep?"

"Rooster getting a wrecker to bring it to the station. Pick it up there this afternoon."

The police car turned down a long, wooded lane that circled around a hill, stretching two miles. The car stopped at a gate with the old man's initials made out of elephant tusk. Scratch dreaded it. Riding along with Shep and Ralph was OK. Talking to Shep was always good. Any time spent inside the mansion, or in the old man's presence, turned Scratch's stomach upside-down.

The guard opened the gates, waved the police car through. He looked miserable, too. As a matter of fact, most of Spiff's employees looked miserable, except Shep and Ralph. That's because they only saw him when they were called in. The butler let them in. Cecil said Spiff was out back shooting skeets. Cecil had been a vet of World War One and carried a shrapnel scar on his chin. He was a lean old man who looked like he'd been an athlete at one time. He knew Spiff's old man from a long time ago. Rumor had it, they rode together before World War One and may have robbed a few banks out in New Mexico. They were chased by a posse and Cecil was shot, left for dead. A few months later, Spiff's father showed up and busted Cecil out. By then though, Spiff's father had claimed all the money and left Cecil with zip. A broken man, he became subordinate to Spiff's father – a slave and an employee.

Wonderful to have friends, right?

Spiff was out by the lake he had built last spring, playing skeets. His gruff bellow announcing, "Pull!" didn't jibe with nature. No birds were singing, and even the ripples on the lake were quiet. The blast from the shotgun disrupted Scratch's thoughts, too. He had to close his eyes and quickly think of something else. The sound of gunfire took him back to that mountain in Korea. For the most part, Spiff was terrible at skeets, he would only hit one plate out of five.

When he hit a plate, he acted overconfident, looking at his lawyer, Dan Lowery, like it was meant for Spiff to be the best at everything.

When he missed, he cursed and stomped his feet like an oversized child.

"See that?" Spiff said to Lowery.

"Yes sir." the young man in a powder-blue suit tugged at his tie and adjusted his glasses.

"That's how you do it, Lowery!" Spiff chuckled. "You can learn a lot from an old coot like me."

"Yes sir." Lowery acted as if he was too scared to say anything else but yes sir.

Spiff was still in his pajamas. He often did that. Went to lunches, or in town to shop. Even went to business meetings and board meetings in his nightwear. No one knew exactly why.

"If it isn't the Three Stooges," Spiff said.

Shep wasn't amused. He kept a sour demeanour when he was around Spiff. Keeping it all business curtailed the abuse. Might have been one of the reasons Shep was the only one Spiff had any respect for.

"Let's get this over with, old man," Shep said. "I got some fishing to do."

"Don't you have a county to protect? You're always fishing or hunting," Spiff retorted.

"I have to relax somehow after dealing with you," Shep said.

Spiff smiled. He liked that. The bantering and the way Shep stood up to him.

"How about you?" The old man asked Ralph.

"I don't understand the question, sir," Ralph said.

"You going home to diddle the little lady?"

Ralph didn't like that. He didn't like it at all.

"Make some more children you can't afford to have?"

"Yes sir," Ralph said. "A whole clan. So one day they can take this godforsaken town from you and make it decent," Ralph snarled and turned to Shep: "I'll wait in the car." He walked to the car, looked behind him every step of the way.

The old man laughed. Everyone around the old man felt uncomfortable. But he was king of his world and he showed it. He instructed Lowery to pour him a whiskey sour out of the pitcher sitting on a tray beside two folding chairs. Shep decided to sit in one of the chairs. He sighed as he sat down slowly.

Lowery handed Spiff a tall glass and the old man snatched it from him aggressively.

Scratch wanted to hurry back to the police station to get his car. He had business at the Primrose. He kicked at a stick on the ground.

"You antsy, boy," Spiff drained his glass. "You got something on your mind?"

"I want to get the hell out of here," Scratch said. "I need to find out who's trying to set me up."

"Leave it alone, yardbird," Spiff told him. "You're out of the fire. Don't jump back into another?"

"What's that mean?" Scratch asked.

"Don't screw with it, is what it means. I'm not tellin' ya, I'm ordering ya!"

Spiff and Scratch locked eyes.

"I don't have to work for you," Scratch said.

Spiff chuckled. "Oh yeah you do, yardbird. Nothin' anywhere else for you. No one's gonna take a broken-down GI who has nightmares while wide awake. So stop fuckin' around and pay attention to young Lowery. He has something for you to do at Horace Hammock's house."

"Why not send Shep?"

"Because you're the yardbird, boy. He's the sheriff. He's busy protecting the county."

"And your interests," Scratch said.

Spiff sniffed the air. "It's the same damn thing."

"Yes, Scratch. There's something Mr Spiff would like you to get from Horace Hammock's house," Lowery said.

He'd fixed himself a smaller glass of whiskey and poured a shot of freshly squeezed orange juice in it. Scratch had never seen anyone make an alcoholic drink with orange juice. Lowery cleared his throat and continued.

"It's a large 13-inch black vinyl hatbox with a gold satin rope around it. Gold initials on the front: SS."

"And the significance of this hatbox?" Scratch asked.

"Don't worry about it!" Spiff screamed before Lowery had a chance to answer. The old man's spit went all over Shep, who jumped from his chair, cursing. Lowery flashed an uneasy smile. Spiff continued his tirade. "Stop asking dumb questions and do what yardbirds do!"

"What is it I'm supposed to do, huh?" Scratch retorted. He was hot under the collar. Sick of the old man ordering him around. Sick of the uppity attitudes of a hick town like Odarko. He just wanted to go back to Darktown. Back to where people acted like real people and not characters from a Robert Mitchum movie.

"Yardbirds do what I tell 'em to do! Nothing more! You gotta eat, I tell ya! You gotta sleep, I tell ya! Ya gotta take a shit…" Spiff chuckled, "…I definitely tell ya to shit. Now, get, boy. I'm sick of seein' ya!"

8

Shep and Ralph took Scratch to the Wildwood Diner. He didn't eat much. He didn't say much. He had a lot on his mind. Afterwards, they dropped him off at the station to get his car.

He was torn about what to do first. He knew he needed to go back to the room at the Primrose before they cleaned it up, but he'd been ordered to get a hatbox from Horace Hammock's house. Was it the same hatbox? He couldn't remember. Some of what happened in that room was kind of shaky in his memory. Scratch wasn't sure if it was because of wallop on the head or because the nightmares were of Korea were haunting him again.

Scratch started his '48 Dodge and eased out of the parking space. He put the car into drive, rolled down Main Street slowly, then took a quick right on Tulip drive. He was going to Horace Hammock's house first. Twilight was setting in and the moon and the sun were exchanging hellos and goodbyes. Scratch came up on a stop sign and he jabbed at the car brakes, tires squealing.

A three-story brick house sat at the end of Tulip. Horace Hammock's house.

Scratch parked at the end of the street. Then he cut through a little wooded area that led past three other people's houses before he reached the backyard of Horace's house. He crept past several hedges that hadn't been trimmed in months, and circled around a shack that was ready to fall apart at the first whisper of noise. He came to the high window of what looked to be a study.

Scratch saw a tall brown-haired woman in oval-shaped glasses, red blouse and black skirt, rifling through a chestnut desk. She was being fast and sloppy. Tossing papers aside, books, old newspaper clippings and photographs. The woman was actually quite striking, thick-boned with an hourglass shape. Scratch was immediately attracted to her. She took him back to the days when he fancied a school teacher he had as a teenager. He watched her a little longer, and when she gave up irritably and sat on a small couch in the study, Scratch decided to go inside the house himself.

He jimmied the lock on the backdoor with the fingernail file on his Swiss Army Knife. The lock popped with no trouble and Scratch opened the backdoor carefully. He went through the kitchen, felt his way through the darkness, using a light in the hallway as a guide. From the hallway, the living room was dark, but the light from the study was shining through the door left partly open. Scratch saw the woman's leg and her shoeless stockinged foot hanging off the couch. Scratch pushed the door with the palm of his hand and the door creaked open.

The woman turned her head and stared at Scratch with tired eyes. She was now sitting upright but with her legs stretched along on the couch. Both shoes were off her feet and her brown hair was loose about her shoulders, not pulled up in a bun as it had been when he last saw her. The first few buttons on her blouse were unfastened and its collar was loose and wide, revealing a long white neckline and even more of a see-through diamond-patterned brassiere.

Her eyes grew large and she quickly reached into her purse and pulled out a small .22 gold plated Luger. She got to her feet swiftly. She was like a tiger, graceful, fast and apparently just as dangerous. Her dark eyes screwed down in a squint and her upper lip caught the wave of a curl that seemed so popular once a certain entertainer burst on the scene.

"Hold it right there, buster!" She spoke fast, too, like the heroine of one of those screwball comedies from the thirties.

"Easy, sister," Scratch said. "No reason to let that thing go off."

"I will, if you make any sudden moves," the woman said.

"No sudden moves from me," Scratch said.

"Who are you?" She demanded.

"Sheriff Shep Howard," Scratch said.

The woman was taken aback and not fully certain whether that was a lie or the truth.

"Where's your badge?" She asked.

Scratch shrugged. "At the station."

"Well," she said, exasperated. "I don't understand..."

"What I'm doing isn't exactly legal."

"Police do it all the time," she said. "Breaking into houses... Say, what's with the patch over your eye?"

"A burglar shot it out a few years ago," Scratch said.

Again, the woman didn't know whether to believe him or not. She grunted an OK. "Why are you here?"

Scratch took a step toward her. The woman raised her eyebrows and shook her head at him. Scratch smiled and said: "I forgot something here when we answered the call to the suicide of Mr Hammock."

"Suicide?" The woman lowered the Luger slightly, her wrist tiring from holding it in the same position. "He didn't commit suicide."

"No?" Scratch asked.

"No! He was stabbed in the back of the neck... Wait! Shouldn't you know this if you're the Sheriff?"

Scratch lunged at her and caught the woman's hand just as the Luger went off. He forced her hand toward the floor. The bullet struck the floorboard by her left foot. She screamed, jumped, and dropped the gun. Scratch was already falling on top of the woman, grabbing the collar of her blouse.

The material ripped as he and the woman fell hard on the floor. He was lying on top of her, face to face. She was struggling with him, her skirt riding up and her legs wrapped around his waist, revealing the same diamond pattern panties, black garter belt attached to suntan stockings. She tore a hand free and dug her nails into Scratch's right cheek. He groaned and took hold of the hand, forcing it to the floor to match the other he already had pinned down.

Her eyeglasses were pulled to one side and he got a good look at big brown eyes.

"Wow," he found himself saying without realizing it. "You really are a knockout."

This statement caught the woman by surprise.

The woman gasped. "I… I am?"

There was an uneasy silence. they both gave a nervous laugh. Scratch did the gentlemanly thing. He removed himself from the woman, even though the next logical step would have been to kiss her. She seemed torn between wanting him to stay and fixing her skirt to a more presentable position.

Scratch sat up and leaned against the couch. The woman joined him. She fixed her glasses, then her hair. Scratch took out a pack of Camels and offered her a cigarette. She smiled and took it between her first and middle fingers.

"I suppose I should introduce myself," she said. "I'm Lilly Griffin. I'm Mr Hammock's secretary – was his secretary."

Scratch smiled, tipped his hat up. He lit her cigarette first, then his. They blew out smoke simultaneously.

"Yeah, well, I'm not the sheriff," Scratch said.

Lilly cocked her head. "I gathered that." She chortled. "Did someone really shoot your eye out?"

"No." Scratch laughed. "Lost it in a car accident."

"Oh." Lilly was disappointed. She wanted to hear a good, action-packed story, and she would've been OK with a lie. "So who are you then?"

"My name is Scratch Williams." He inhaled then exhaled blue smoke. "I work for Oliver Spiff."

"Ah," Lilly said. "That makes sense."

"How so?"

She took a long drag from her cigarette and gazed at Scratch for 45 seconds or longer, before exhaling. A huge cloud of blue smoke rose to the air above her head. Scratch watched the smoke disappear, then shifted his eyes back to Lilly's. She had a thin top lip and rather full bottom lip, and Scratch noticed Lilly had painted on her red lipstick to make the top lip look as full the bottom. Still, Scratch really liked her appearance. He thought she was striking, with those gold-tinged, slightly thick brown eyebrows and thin, spider-web lashes.

"Spiff and Horace hated each other. But they needed each other," Lilly said. "Horace went bankrupt a few years back. Borrowed money from Spiff. Spiff thought he owned the newspaper. Fat chance," she shook her head and laughed. "No way, José. Horace made a deal with someone in Vegas. He paid Spiff back every penny. Tore up the marker in his face."

"Is that what's in the hatbox?" Scratch asked.

Lilly shrugged. "What hatbox?"

"That's what you're looking for," Scratch said.

"No I'm not."

"Then why do you look so guilty?"

"Look, buster..." She turned red in the face and her anger level had risen to 10. That top lip started to curl up again.

Scratch was pleased with himself for that accomplishment. He threw his hands up, smiling. "OK, OK. You're not looking for a hatbox."

"Good! I'm glad we got that out of the way!"

He had another question designed to make her even angrier. One of Scratch's favorite pastimes was getting under people's skins. He really enjoyed needling them. Sticking it to them and seeing what the outcome was. If the situation became ugly, he'd apologize or wait for the first punch to be thrown. Afterwards, retaliate anyway he could.

"So..." He chose his words carefully. "You call him 'Horace' and not 'Mr Hammock?'"

Instead of getting mad, Lilly smiled.

Scratch threw another fireball at her. "Were you more than just his secretary?"

She batted those huge eyelashes at Scratch, the spider web dashed the lens of her eyeglasses with light-speed precision.

"Of course I was," Lilly said. "Just not in public or in his bed," she sighed. "He'd take me from behind at his desk once a week. Or he did. Until I hit 30. Then it became less frequent. More like every couple months. Does that shock you?"

Scratch smiled, shook his head slowly. "No," he said. "I was thinking what a lucky man he was."

Lilly laughed, batted her eyes and touched her hair, embarrassed.

"Did you love him?" Scratch asked.

"God, no," Lilly made a face. "No one in their right mind would love a person like Horace. I did some digging on Horace Hammock a few years ago, when a blackmail letter came to the office. His real name was Leon Goldman. A New York City reporter, who left behind two wives and six children. Left them destitute. A young man had delivered that letter. There was an exchange of money. He went away. I think he was Horace's son. So, I'll say it again. No one could love a sorry bastard like that. Not even that bimbo he was sleeping with who was 40 years younger than him."

"Bimbo, huh?" Scratch said. "This bimbo have a name?"

"Caroline Seafront. She's barely 21. Horace has been with her for a year or so. You've seen her around town, I'm sure. Blonde, big blue eyes, even bigger tits."

Scratch laughed.

"What?" Lilly laughed with him. "A woman can't talk dirty?"

Scratch shrugged. "No. I mean, I don't mind so much. It's just… "

"Just what?" Lilly had to get the bottom of the look on Scratch's face and the shrug.

"Just… it doesn't go with your demeanor."

"What's my demeanor?"

Scratch waited to answer. "You remind me of a school teacher I had."

"Oh," she sounded disappointed with his answer. Or hurt. "Or a librarian. Either way, I remind you of a lonely spinster."

"No," Scratch said. "A school teacher I wanted to bed."

The smile returned to Lilly's face. "Is that what you want to do? Take me to bed?"

"No," Scratch said.

The smile disappeared.

"I want to bend you over that desk," Scratch said.

The smile returned. Lilly slowly stood. Contemplated slipping into her heels, but decided against it. She walked over to the desk, bent over and lifted her skirt over her waist. She eased her hands to her ass, pulled down those diamond-pattern panties. The roundness of her cheeks reminded Scratch of a huge ivory ball, and it made the garter belt flex out and her stockings ride up and expand.

Smiling, she looked over her shoulders at him.

"Well?" Lilly asked. "What are you waiting for?"

9

Lilly excused herself to go to the bathroom. She was gone for quite a bit. Scratch decided to see if Horace had any beer in the icebox. Sure enough, two bottles of Blue Ribbon sat not far from a dish of cold cuts. Scratch took down a plate. He fixed a sandwich for himself and Lilly. He carried the plate and the beer with him as he searched for Lilly.

She wasn't in the bathroom anymore. The light was on, but the door was wide open. By now, the Grandfather clock in the living room said it was nine forty-five. He searched the study. Lilly wasn't there. He searched the guest bedroom. She wasn't there either. Scratch went upstairs.

Hanging around the top of the stair, in the hallway, he heard Lilly in the bedroom on the left. Scratch made as little noise as he drew closer to the partly open door. He peaked inside. That bedroom belonged to woman. Lilly had tossed clothing everywhere. Dresses lay on a canopy bed. Undergarments and stockings on the floor beside dresser drawers. Lilly sat on the bed, crossed her legs angrily – obviously upset she hadn't found what she was looking for.

But she wasn't dissuaded.

Struck by a thought, she uncrossed her legs and jumped from the bed. She reached behind the bedpost and dug down. She smiled. Lilly had found what she was looking for. She pulled it out slowly. A white silk blouse was wrapped around a ball of newspapers. She unwrapped the blouse, tossed it aside. She unpeeled the newspaper carefully and discovered what looked to be three stacks of ten 20- dollar bills, bound by paper bands.

Lilly clasped her hands together, threw her head back and cackled.

When she came downstairs, she found Scratch sitting on the couch, eating and watching television. She wandered over and sat beside him, casting a leg over his. They grinned at each other.

"I made you something to eat," he said. "Got you a beer, too."

"How sweet," Lilly said. "Thank you." She snatched the sandwich from the plate and bit into it like a rabid dog. Scratch watched her eat, finding it humorous she ate as sloppily as he did.

"Here's your beer," he offered the bottle.

Lilly shook her head, picked up Scratch's bottle and drank from it. "That's OK." She gulped and smacked her lips. "I'll have some of yours."

The TV flickered. A cowboy rode through brush and came up on a ranch.

"What are you watching?" Lilly asked.

"Studio One," Scratch kept his eyes on the screen. "But it looks like a cowboy flick. I don't know. I guess the show is trying something different than people arguing with each other in their kitchens."

"I wouldn't know," Lilly said. "I only watch *Our Miss Brooks*."

Scratch gazed at Lilly. That was it, he thought. He couldn't put his finger on it before. Now he knew. She did resemble Eve Arden. Did she purposely try to make herself look like the actress? Yeah, Scratch told himself. She did. He nodded. Eve Arden was a knockout, he told himself.

"What?" Lilly asked, making a face, shifting that full bottom lip to the side.

"Nothing," Scratch said. After a few minutes he blurted out: "I think we should go back to my place."

Lilly laughed. "You do, do you?"

"Yeah," he said, and kissed her softly. "I do."

"Well," she said, pulling away, "I-I can't."

"Oh. Why not?"

Lilly waited to answer. She was trying to come up with a good excuse.

"I don't know," she said, looking away. "I... just shouldn't."

"Shouldn't or don't want to?"

Lilly shrugged.

"A little of both," she said, removing her leg from Scratch's. She fixed her skirt.

"OK," he said.

There was complete silence for a good while. The grandfather clock chimed, alerting them to the fact the time was eleven o'clock.

"I... guess I'll get going." Lilly stood.

"Why didn't you tell me about the money?"

"What are you talking about?"

"The money you found," Scratch said. "Three stacks of 20s, held together with paper bands."

"I don't know what you're talking about!" Lilly protested. Her hands immediately went to her waist. The torn collar fell, and showed even more of her cleavage and brassiere. As a matter of fact, the erect nipple of her left breast was out from the top of the cup. That top lip curled up once more.

"The money." Scratch stood. Lilly took a step back from him. "The money you found behind the bed, in the upstairs bedroom on the left. The bedroom you tossed, looking for *that money*. The money. I know you have it. Where is it, Lilly?"

"I don't have any money!" she said, voice strained, higher pitched, through clenched teeth.

Scratch pushed Lilly on to the couch. They struggled as he fell on top of her, his hands all over her, searching, her hands swatting his away. He pushed her skirt up and saw the bills tucked away in both of her stocking tops. One stack inside her left stocking, two stacks in her right. Lilly dug her nails in his hand, tried to keep him from her legs. It didn't work. Scratch was determined to take the money, no matter what. Her high heels fell from her feet. She unsuccessfully kicked at his face, missing when he dodged from side to side. He finally held her legs down, palms pressing her thighs to the couch. Lilly squealed and gave Scratch a left hook, connecting to his chin. He fell on the floor, touching his agonizingly painful chin.

"Damn," Scratch said. "You pack a wallop!"

"And don't forget it, buster!" Lilly screamed, fixing her skirt. She sat up on the couch, snarling at him. She found her heels and stepped in them. "I'm going to go now."

"Wait," Scratch begged her, touching her leg. "Please... I need your help." He massaged her ankle, moved up to her knee under the skirt. "I need your help." She let out a small sigh. "You obviously know every inch of this house," he said. "Please help me find that hatbox. I can't go back to Spiff without it." His hand moved up her thigh and to her panties, gently rubbing. A longer sigh came from her parted lips. Her eyes became glassy, looking past Scratch. Scratch's fingers kept rubbing, quicker and quicker until Lilly cried out, spread her legs and moaned.

After a few minutes, she got herself together and caught her breath. She swallowed hard, and nodded. "Yeah." Lilly breathed out. "I'll help you."

* * *

Lilly helped Scratch look for the hatbox. They turned over every room. The hatbox was in the bathroom. Under the sink. It was black, but no gold trim, and no initials, especially SS. Lilly was overjoyed. She cried out and ran to Scratch. She threw her arms around his neck and kissed him.

Scratch was confused. That was not the hatbox Lowery or the old man described. This hatbox was old, the black vinyl faded and chipped.

"We found it!" Lilly gushed. She kissed Scratch, exploring his mouth with her tongue. She pulled away and said: "I plan on sharing the money with you."

Scratch smiled. He appreciated the gesture, but knew more than likely she would hang on to it for him.

"Thank you," he said.

"I'm... just going to hold on to your share. OK, baby?"

Scratch laughed. "OK."

Lilly was a little perturbed that Scratch found the offer humorous. That top lip started to curl up.

"What?" she asked.

"Nothing," Scratch said. He put his hands on her shoulders and kissed her. She pulled away.

"No. There is something."

Scratch kissed her again. Lilly gave in. Her anger subsided. After the long kiss, Lilly rested her head on Scratch's chest. They walked out the bathroom like that, hand in hand, to the front door of the house. Lilly moved snuggled to Scratch, moved her head to his shoulder.

"Let's go to my place," Scratch said. "Get some rest."

Out of the corner of his eye, Scratch saw a young, light-skinned black male at the window. He was short, wore a checkered button-down shirt and dungarees. His hair was light brown and a little kinky, but relaxed. There was no expression on his haunted face. His eyes looked dead, hollow. By the time Scratch turned to get a full view, the man was pointing a Saturday night special at Lilly.

The barrel of the gun was bigger than the man's head. Scratch pushed Lilly to the floor just as the gun discharged.

"Get out of the way!" He screamed and jumped toward the couch.

Lilly fell on her back. The bullet zipped past both of them and struck a lamp, tore a hole in the shade and burrowed into the wall. Scratch jumped to his feet. He flung the front door open and ran after the young man. In his younger days, Scratch had been fast, but not as fast this little man.

The man was several blocks ahead of Scratch, leading the way down Main Street, past all the shops, Mildred's hair shop and Gus's barber. The man took a right down an alley just off Smith lane that led to the back of Hamilton's greengrocer. Scratch hung in there, still far behind the man, until the chase led to a path and a hill to the park. Scratch's knee gave out.

He found himself lying on wet grass, staring at the bright yellow moon, trying to catch his breath. He lifted himself up and watched the young man sprint into the woods that led to Jennings Farm, then disappear into the darkness.

"Son of a bitch." Scratch huffed and puffed. He lay there for several moments.

When he was ready to stand, he used the dead roots of a long-gone tree to prop himself up. He hobbled through the park, on to Main Street and back to Horace Hammock's house, where Lilly was waiting nervously on the couch. Scratch limped inside, holding his knee.

"What happened? Did he shoot you?" She trotted to Scratch, her heels clicking repetitively like bongo drums. She helped him to the couch, her hands on his waist and back, his resting on her shoulders.

"No," Scratch shook his head. "I chased him all the way to the park. My knees gave out on me. Don't worry, Lilly. I'll find him. He was aiming for you. At first, I thought it was me. But chasing him, thinking about it, I realized he was gunnin' for you."

"I don't know, Scratch," She eased him on to the couch and sat beside him. "Maybe we should let it go."

"I'm not going to do that," Scratch said.

Lilly sighed. "I think its best you do... at-at least for now. So, uh, why don't we go home – you go to your place, and I'll go to mine. I'm awful tired, Scratch. I need a bath and to – you know – relax in my own... space. Oh, don't look that way. Please."

"No, no. I should be around to protect you in case he tries again. I'll go with you..."

"No, Scratch!"

He stared at her.

"Hey," Lilly rubbed his hand. "I'll be OK. That guy is more than likely hiding out somewhere and won't try again. Ever."

"I don't know about that," Scratch said. "He had a look of determination on his face. Why would anyone want to kill you, Lilly?"

"I don't know, Scratch," Lilly said. She ran a hand through her hair. "Can we talk about this tomorrow? I'm dog tired."

Scratch nodded. "Yeah. Sure. We can talk tomorrow. Where? Your home? Hammock's office?"

"No, not my home. Nor Horace's office. That's been closed. Sheriff's orders. How about Jesse Fulton's diner. Out by Newberry."

"On route 10?"

"Yes," Lilly stood. She was in a hurry to leave. Her steps quickened to the front door. She turned the knob, and said: "Is 11am OK? I'm going to sleep in. Hope you don't mind? Me leaving?" Lilly flashed a smile.

"No. I don't mind. You need me to drop you off..?"

"I have my car." She stepped out and, just before she closed the door, she said: "I'll see you tomorrow."

Will you? Scratch asked himself. He looked at the coffee table. The hatbox was gone. He realized Lilly had taken it. "Son of a bitch!"

10

Scratch was tired. He sat in his '48 Dodge for a half hour or so, tried to get himself motivated to drive. First he had to decide where to go. He wanted to go home, to his bed. Fix something to eat. Then he would be fresh in the morning to meet Lilly.

"Ah, who am I kidding?" he asked himself under his breath. "She won't show up tomorrow."

He turned the key in the ignition and the engine started up. The moon was so bright. So yellow. It was like a spotlight. Scratch wished it was all darkness so he could hide. He looked up, watched the stars and that bright moon dance around each other.

He decided to go to the Primrose first. It was on his way to Mrs Howard's house, where he rented the basement.

"No sleep tonight," he said and put the car in drive.

Suddenly, a man ran across the road and slammed into the car. He didn't fall down or scream. Anyway, the car didn't hit him very hard. He just stood there, both hands on the hood. Scratch realized it was the short, light-skinned black man who had shot at Lilly and him. They locked eyes and Scratch rose from the car seat, but a flash of flames caught his eyes.

In the distance, a car radio could be heard playing *Why Do Fools Fall in Love?*

Scratch turned to look, as did the young man. A burning cross appeared about six houses down. That house belonged to a young Mexican family, that much Scratch knew. The young man had come run-ning from that direction. *Uh-oh*, Scratch thought. *The Klan saw him.*

Torches were coming toward them. Voices were hurling all kinds of racial slurs and insults. The young man took off in a sprint. Instinc-tively, Scratch sped off. He almost collided with a familiar car – a red Plymouth Fury. *Why Do Fools Fall in Love?* was at its loudest. The Fury skidded to the left and barely missed a fire hydrant. The Dodge skidded to the right, knocking over a public trashcan. The driver hung his head out the window. The young blond-haired man had a mali-cious upturned smile on his thin face. Scratch had seen him driving off from the drugstore the day before. In the passenger and backseat were two women. Scratch couldn't make out who they were, nor did he have time. The torches were getting closer. Scratch hit the gas and the Dodge sped off again.

"Why am I running?" Scratch said out loud. "They're not after me." He pulled the car over and parked by Nesbit's hardware store.

About 10 men in white robes and pointed hoods, carrying torches, ran past Hammock's house. The embers from the flames surged and left a trail of remnants as the white robes dashed past the Dodge. The man led them by three paces, but that was dwindling with Klansman hot on his heels.

They all whooped and hollered at the young man. He tripped, fell on his side, and quickly hopped to his feet. He removed the pistol from his belt, pointed it at the white sheets. Too frightened to pull the trigger, he dropped the gun and sprinted toward the park.

"You can't run, nigger!" a gravelly voiced man called out.

"The moon is bright tonight, nigger!" A high-pitched voice called. "You can't hide now, shine!"

"You're gonna wish your mama never had you, boy!"

The Fury sped off, tires squealing.

"Shit," Scratch said. Suddenly, he had a case of the "I cares" and guilt was settling in.

He put the car in drive and tapped the gas pedal. The Dodge sped off and circled in front of the gang of Klansman. The fender struck the gravelly voiced one on his right side. He cried out. The rest of the Klan spread out and Scratch let the Dodge spin around a few times. They regrouped when Scratch stopped, began beating his hood with baseball bats.

Two Klansman men trotted over to help the gravel-voiced one to his feet.

"Get in!" Scratch screamed at the young man.

The man pulled the handle, and the back door on the passenger's side popped open. He dove into the backseat. Scratch sped off, tires squealing. The door, still open, clipped one of the charging Klansman, knocking him to the ground. Scratch's passenger grabbed the door handle and slammed the door shut. He lay back down, closed his eyes, and let out a sigh of relief.

Insults, rocks and baseball bats were hurled at the Dodge. Scratch didn't waste any time driving through Odarko. He hurried to route 10, headed to Bucksville. The moon showed the way, and there were rows and rows of trees on the side of the road, along with white lines on the highway, that hypnotized Scratch. He felt his eyelids getting heavier and heavier, and the faces of George Spiff, Shep Howard and Lilly kept invading his mind. The Dodge veered to the right. The front tire nearly hit a ditch. Scratch's passenger was not happy about being rescued, nor his driving ability.

"Hey! Wake up!" The man yelled.

Scratch jerked awake and steered the Dodge back on the road.

"You can let me out here, OK?"

"I'm not letting you out," Scratch told the man.

"C'mon, now. What are you doing? Kidnapping me?"

"No," Scratch said. "Just holding you against your will."

"What?" The man protested, thought about what Scratch said. "Hey, man, that's the same thing!"

"Hmm, is it? Whatever it's called, boy, I'm doing it. You're going to answer some questions, then I'm taking you to see Shep Howard."

"Who the hell is that?"

"Sheriff around these parts," Scratch said.

"Hey… I'm-I'm grateful for you picking me up before the hoods could string me up, but I ain't going to no white lawman," the man said. "I could wind up beat all to all to hell, meetin' Jesus when I wake up. No way, José."

"You'll be safer in a cell…"

"The hell you say! Look… just let me out."

"I'll take you to Darktown. How's that?"

"You ain't allowed in there any more than I'm allowed in Odarko," the man said.

"You'll be surprised when they open the gates to let me in," Scratch said. "First you're going to answer some questions."

"I ain't answerin' shit," the man said.

"You'll answer them," Scratch said. "Or I'll turn this car around and drop you off where those Klansman were having a barbecue."

The man didn't reply. Complete silence for a bit, until Scratch reiterated his reasons for rescuing the man.

"What's your name?"

The man didn't answer.

Scratch nodded.

"That's OK. I can find that out. Why did you try to kill the woman in that house?"

"Look, I-I didn't want to, OK?" he sighed. "This guy… he came in to Darktown. He…" The man was hesitant, embarrassed. "He wanted some company."

"Company? What do you mean?"

The man clucked his tongue.

"What do you think I mean?"

Scratch looked over his shoulder at the man. "Oh. Yeah. You look like a sissy."

"I ain't no sissy! I'm as touch as they come! You saw me with that gun!"

Scratch chuckled. "Yeah," he said sarcastically and moved his eyes back to the road. "OK, buddy. You're tough. What did this man look like?"

The young man shrugged. "A white man."

"What did he look like?" Scratch repeated the question with more aggression.

The young man shivered. "I don't know! I-I don't usually remember things like that... especially if I'd been smokin'... You know, been in a cloud..."

"Then what?"

"We did some stuff," the man said. "Hey... you ain't a weirdo who pulls on himself while I talk dirty, are you?"

"What the hell?" Scratch laughed, looked at the man incredulously.

"Anyways, after all that, the guy gives me a package. A gun, 200 dollars and an address. He says: 'Go to any window, you see a man there, shoot him!' I said: 'I ain't never killed nobody.' It ain't been my chance yet but it... it's comin' up... and I ain't lookin' forward to it. Anyways, he says: 'Do this, and I'll throw in another 200.' Shit...." The man laughed. "I ain't never seen 200 dollars, let alone 400 at one time. I told him I'd kill the mayor for that amount. He said: 'Maybe another time.' Shit... I'll take him up on it."

"So, you were aiming for me?" Scratch asked.

The man shrugged. "I was aimin' for anybody to collect that other 200."

"You can't tell me what this guy looked like?"

"No," the man smiled, showing two bottom teeth that had rotted out. "I can. But I won't. Unless you flash some green."

"I can pay you," Scratch said. The man got even happier, danced in the backseat. Scratch hit the brakes and the car came to halt. The man fell forward, his face smashed into the hard vinyl seat in front of him. The man screamed out.

"But I won't," Scratch said.

Scratch turned the engine off.

"What are you doin'?" The man asked.

"I think I'll just beat the information out of you," Scratch said calmly.

The man popped the back door open and jumped out before Scratch could open the car door. The man hit the hard pavement and yelped.

He rolled off the road and into a ditch. He sprang to his feet and dashed towards the woods. The man disappeared into the dark woods.

"Damn it!" Scratch slammed the palm of his hand on the car roof.

11

He was gone. Nothing Scratch could do about that. But he could ride into Darktown and see Immy and Dobro. Before that, he needed to go back to his place and get cleaned up. His head was swimming. Maybe a shower and some food would help.

Truth be told, Scratch needed some sleep. Only, he was afraid if he laid down, he'd have that nightmare again. He'd wake up out in the streets at two in the morning, that .38 in his hands looking for Korean soldiers. In the last few months, since that incident, Scratch had avoided sleep as much as possible. But there are times a person can't. The body shuts down.

He stood on Mrs Howard's lawn. He saw a light was still on in the ranch-style house. The moon still shining brightly showed the lime green house and white roof. He saw a hand move black drapes and an elderly woman with dyed blonde hair peeked out. Scratch wasn't in the mood to talk to his landlady.

Scratch liked her. He liked her a lot. She was motherly. Sometimes too much to the point it was annoying. He was grateful to Shep for suggesting to his cousin, Lenora Howard, that she should rent her basement to him. But that night, and the time being one thirty in the morning, she needed to go to bed and not poke her nose in Scratch's business, like she normally did. He rushed off toward the steps that lead to the door of his basement apartment.

After his shower, Scratch was getting dressed. He had to sit down for a minute. He sat on his bed, basically just a cot with a sheet, blanket and one flat pillow. Next thing he knew, he'd dozed off, still sitting up. There was a knock on the door. A gentle rapping was more like it. The knock startled Scratch.

He sprang from his bed, looked around the room. The knocking continued and there was a voice.

"Mr Williams?" Mrs Howard's voice was faint through the closed door.

Scratch didn't want to open the door. He wasn't in the mood. Mrs Howard meant well. He knew that. She doted on Scratch like the son she never had. Again, Scratch was not in the mood for her. Still, it was her house.

Scratch opened the door and the old woman appeared in the doorway, looking apprehensive. She was in a black and white floral kimono and she held the top of it closed with one hand while she flashed an envelope with the other.

"Hello, Mrs Howard," Scratch said.

"Hello, Mr Williams. I was coming down to give you this letter. As I was coming down the steps, I heard you scream. Are you all right?"

Scratch chuckled. "Yes, Mrs Howard. I... uh, this is embarrassing..." He was trying to make something up. He didn't want to say he was dreaming. She'd never leave. She'd offer to make him dinner and coax him upstairs to have tea and a talk. "I slammed the bathroom cabinet on my hand. I'm so clumsy." Scratch chuckled again.

"Ohh, you poor thing." Mrs Howard invited herself in. Had a quick look around to see if a woman was there. That was one of her pet peeves. She mentioned it almost every time she saw Scratch when he first moved in. "Why don't you come upstairs and I'll fix you some dinner? Have you had any yet? I bet you haven't?"

"No, no. I'm good. Actually, I had some with Shep earlier."

"Oh, wonderful! Steven is such a good man. How about some tea?" Mrs Howard said.

"I can't. I'm working on something… with Shep. He's going to meet me somewhere."

"Oh! That's too bad! You boys work so hard protecting the community. Maybe one day Shep will make you his deputy," Mrs Howard gasped when another thought came to her. "Or you can be Sheriff when Steven retires! That would be wonderful!"

"Yeah," Scratch laughed. "Maybe one day."

Fat chance, he thought. The old man will never let that happen.

Mrs Howard turned toward the door. "I'll let you finish dressing. I put some fresh shirts in the top drawer of the bureau. I washed and ironed them yesterday morning."

"Thank you, Mrs Howard," Scratch said, holding the door for her.

She went out, then turned quickly. "Oh! Your letter! I almost forgot." She handed it to Scratch. Just a plain envelope with Scratch Williams written on it.

Scratch took the envelope gingerly. "Thank you."

"Well," Mrs Howard said sadly, "I'll say good night."

Scratch smiled. "Good night, Mrs Howard."

"Good night, Mr Williams."

He watched her take the first step, then the second slowly. She looked over her shoulder at Scratch. He closed the door to send a signal the conversation was over.

Scratch ripped the envelope open. He sighed. *What now?* He thought. A sheet of plain white typewriter paper was inside.

Scratch took it out and smelled the paper. Brand new. Just out of a pack. He unfolded it. Read the typed message, made a face, then reread the letter, mouthing the words.

"I know who you really are. I know what you really are. You were born in St Johnson Infirmary in 1934. You are a nigger and you grew up in Darktown. You killed your father and your sister knows. Pay $500.00 and no one will ever know, except you and me. If you don't pay, you will go to the Electric Chair and everyone will know your sister's shame. You know how he feels about your breed. Meet me at

Kemora Lake, around the back side leading into Darktown at 10pm tomorrow."

No signature.

"Five hundred dollars. Who the hell has 500 dollars on their person?"

Something caught Scratch's eye.

Hmm. What's this in the right corner? It was faint, faded. Something printed. A stamp? No. More like a company logo. Whoever sent it tried to erase it.

Scratch thought about it. He smelled the paper again. Wait. That wasn't a new smell.

"Lye soap," he said. "Son of a bitch tried to use lye soap." He touched that corner, felt how brittle it was.

He took the paper to the lamp, removed the shade and held the paper under the glowing, naked light. The print became more evident. Sheriff's office. The letter had been written on a typewriter on paper with the header COLEMAN COUNTY SHERIFF'S OFFICE.

"Shaw wrote this," Scratch said out loud.

He started to crumple the letter, and thought better. He smoothed out the letter, read it once more.

"Son of a bitch calling me a nigger," Scratch said. "I'll show him."

He was already on his way to see Darktown to talk to Dobro. Maybe Scratch would discuss the letter with him.

Scratch went to the icebox, took out a saucer with liverwurst and a jar of mayonnaise. He sat it all on the counter by the sink, opened the bread box and cut two slices. He fixed the sandwich and went out the door, leaving everything sitting on the counter.

12

Scratch didn't exactly miss Darktown. He missed the people. He missed Immy and Dobro. He didn't miss Culke Lowe, the self-professed sheriff of Darktown not recognized by any judicial or state law. He sure as hell didn't miss his uncles, who basically ran Darktown.

The area still looked the way it did in the twenties before electricity hit Oklahoma. Rows and rows of broken-down houses that used to be sharecroppers' homes went on until the horizon turned into woods.

It was way too late to see Immy, but he decided to go to her house anyway. Her kids would be asleep, but last time Scratch spoke to her, Immy had as much trouble sleeping as he did. He went to a small faded green shack that sat among several larger shacks. A big brown four-story house sat behind the shacks. That house belonged to the landlord, Calvin Stevens. He was a miserable old bastard when he could remember who owed rent to him. Immy had in the past had to offer her body to Stevens to pay the rent.

Scratch stepped on the porch and looked through the kitchen window. A gentle breeze blew the drapes and he saw Immy sitting at her kitchen table, reading. A quarter bottle of Carmen Brothers' whiskey sat beside a plate of meatloaf and mashed potatoes.

Scratch knocked lightly. Immy looked up, startled. A huge grin spread across her face. She jumped from the kitchen chair, her nightgown riding up, and trotted barefoot across the linoleum floor to the door. She opened the door and Scratch stepped inside. Nothing was said.

Immy threw her arms around Scratch's neck.

"I missed you, Allan," she said. Scratch hugged her back. "I missed you, too, Sis."

Immy raised an eyebrow, lifted his eye patch. "You wearing your eye patch. Where's the eye?"

"I lost it," Scratch said and smiled. "A long story."

Immy shrugged. "You'll tell me when you're ready." Immy hugged Scratch again. She pulled away, shut the front door and lead Scratch by the hand to the kitchen table.

"Sit down," she said. "You want some meatloaf?"

"Oh, no," Scratch shook his head, sat down. "My stomach is in knots right now."

"Want some coffee?" Immy asked.

He really didn't. Immy was just like their mother. If you kept denying her hospitality, she'd get angry. One thing to consider about both women was they were nice to an extreme, but if you got them riled there was no end to their dissatisfaction with you.

"Yeah, sure," Scratch said.

She filled the coffee pot with water, and spooned coffee into the filter. She gave Scratch a curious look.

"What brings you back to Darktown, brother?"

"Problems," scratch sighed.

"Aren't they always?" Immy said. "You left Odarko with troubles, brought them to Darktown to add to their troubles? Darktown is not going to fix anything for you. You should know that."

"Where's Carter?" scratch asked.

"That shiftless jackass? He left again," Immy said.

"Back to the oil rigs?"

Immy shook her head. "No. Gone for good," she watched the percolator bubble up. "I'm not so sure I'm sad he's gone." She looked up at Scratch. "He reminds me of Daddy."

"Oh, yeah?"

"Yeah. I found out two months ago Carter had another family. Less than a mile from here. Two kids with that poor young girl and she was four months pregnant. That poor girl."

"He go to her?"

"Fat chance," Immy laughed. "That piece of shit can't be tied down, Allan. Just like our piece of shit daddy."

"Yeah," Scratch tried not to think about his father. His mind often drifted back to the man. The things he did right, which weren't many, the things he did wrong, which were countless.

"You had it worse than I did when he was in the house," Immy said. The coffee was ready. Immy poured Scratch a cup, sat it on the table and pushed the sugar toward him. "I'm out of cream."

"I don't use it anyway. I drink it black nowadays," Scratch said.

Immy smiled. "Me too." She sat down, scooted her chair very close to Scratch, placed her head on his shoulder.

"You can't sleep either?" he asked.

"The past keeps haunting me... ghosts root under my skin."

"Yeah." Scratch drank his coffee. "Me too."

"Been thinking about what happened to us. What happened with me and Daddy... what he did to you when you were born. How he thought you were the devil, tried to drown you in the kitchen sink. All of your childhood that son of a bitch called you Mr Scratch because he was sure you were evil and you would bring bad luck to everyone. I hate that damn nickname. Don't you?"

"No." Scratch stared off in the distance. "I try not to think about it," he said. "Any of it."

"You didn't bring me bad luck." Immy snuggled closer to Scratch. "You saved me, brother. More than once. You saved me from him."

Scratch scoffed. "Immy, let's not talk about it."

"We should," she whispered. "It helps me get over it for a little bit. Just... knowing you'll always protect me."

Yeah, Scratch thought. Who's going to protect me?

"How's Micha and Justine?" Scratch asked.

"They miss their Uncle Allan," Immy said. "Micha is reading The Adventures of Robin Hood. He had an idea to steal some fruit from Mr Pitt and give it to the Rodgers twins."

Scratch laughed. "He didn't steal for himself..."

Immy laughed. "Don't start, Allan. Stealing is stealing, no matter how you look at it."

"I know," Scratch said. "I know. His heart is in the right spot."

"Just like his uncle," Immy said.

"What's Justine been up to?"

"She stayed two days with Carter's mama. She's six years old! Started eatin' peanuts and hooked on those silly soap operas," Immy said.

"How does she watch them? You don't have a television," Scratch said.

"See those cardboard boxes?"

"Yeah," Scratch got up and examined three boxes sitting on top each other sideways.

"That's her television," Immy laughed. "The bottom one is the phonograph where she listens to Miles Davis."

Immy chuckled and Scratch joined in. He stopped, looked inside the top box. A piece of white paper lay inside. He reached in and retrieved it. A familiar smell offended his nostrils. Lye soap. He showed the paper to Immy.

She looked away. Embarrassed and ashamed.

"What's this?" Scratch asked.

"I thought I destroyed those letters," Immy said.

"There were more?"

"Yes."

"How many?"

"They been coming regular every month," Immy said. "All saying the same."

"All demanding 500 dollars," Scratch said.

"Yes."

"You've been paying," Scratch reread the letter.

"Twenty a week," Immy said.

"Do you even have 20 dollars to spend?"

"No, Allan. I don't. I'm working at the factory cuttin' up chickens one shift, leaving, coming back for another shift until 10pm and packaging chicken parts. Damn, I hate chicken!"

"You've met this blackmailer?" Scratch asked.

"Nope," Immy shook her head. "I mail the money." She got up, went to her bedroom and returned with an address book. "Send the money here."

"Looks like a PO Box," Scratch said.

"That's exactly what it is," Immy said. She leaned against the living-room wall, her hands behind her back. "I sat in my car, waited to see if anyone picked it up. I waited two hours. I didn't see anyone go to the box."

'I'm not surprised,' Scratch said. "They came the next day or two, I'm sure."

"No," Immy said. "I'm not sure, but I needed gas. So I drove around the corner, got some gas, drove back and I caught a glimpse of a woman leaving the post office. Just before they closed."

"Can you describe her?"

"White," Immy said. "Light-brown hair, glasses. Our age. Reminds me of a schoolteacher we once had," Immy shrugged. "That's all I remember. You've got that same letter?"

Scratch sighed. "Yeah, Immy. I have. Only this person or persons wanted to meet up with me 10pm at the lake. For some reason they think I have the whole sum of 500 dollars. They agreed to you paying a little at a time?"

"They had no choice. I wrote back, explained I didn't have the thing,"

"Why did you pay?"

"Why do you think, Allan?" Immy raised her voice. "I didn't want people to know my daddy fucked me and my brother killed him for it!"

She took a few steps and burst into tears. Scratch consoled her. He put his arms around Immy and she sobbed hard, her cries muffled against his chest. Faint footsteps cut the situation short. Immy pulled away from Scratch. Micha stood in the open area of the dining room. He rubbed his eyes as he softly called out to Immy.

She told the little boy she was OK and took him by the hand back to the bedroom he and his sister slept in.

Scratch sat the table, drank the coffee from a chipped white mug. He read the letter to himself.

"I know who you really are. I know what you really are. You and your father committed a vile sin. Your brother killed your father for that sin. Pay $500.00 and no one will ever know, except you and me. If you don't pay, your brother will go to the electric chair and everyone will know your shame and why. Send the money to PO BOX 445. Instalments are fine."

After a few minutes, Immy came back in the dining room. They stared at each other, trying to read each other's minds like in a science-fiction serial they saw at the movies when they were kids. Finally, Immy spoke.

"What are we going to do?" she asked.

"No more payments," Scratch said.

Immy sighed, tapped her long fingernails on the wooden table. "OK," she said.

"I think I know who is blackmailing us," Scratch said.

"Who?" Immy leaned in closer to her brother.

"Deputy of Coleman County."

"You're talking about Deputy Shaw," Immy said.

"How do you know him, Immy?" She didn't answer him. She looked away. "I asked you how you knew him!" Scratch grabbed Immy's wrists.

"Get the hell off of me!" Immy screamed. She jerked out of his grip, stood and ran to a corner of the room.

Scratch stood. "I'm sorry, Immy." He held his hands up. "I didn't mean to do that. I just... needed an answer that might make a difference to my decision on this matter."

He took a few steps toward Immy. She relented, fell into Scratch's arms. They hugged. She separated from Scratch, wiped her eyes with a hand and went back to the table. Immy fell on to her chair, worn out from everything. She slumped forward and stared at the floor. She couldn't look Scratch in the eyes.

"There was a party in Rockville," Immy said and her eyes moved to see Scratch's reaction. He wasn't judging her now. He was listening intently. "An old beat-up trailer. That damn thing was falling apart, Scratch."

"Rockville? Never heard of that area," Scratch said.

"Used to be called Wisteria," Immy said. "You were in Korea when they changed the name. Some family's son became a senator or something. Bob Rockner."

"OK."

"Anyway, Celeste Holmes asked some of the girls at the factory if we wanted to make some extra money. Well, of course we all did. Who doesn't need money? Except your boss."

Scratch sighed. "Can I go one day without a person mentioning him? What kind of party was this?"

"It was a party. The kind you don't invite your preacher to," Immy said.

"How many girls?"

"Celeste could only get three of us," Immy rubbed her face. "So she had to come, too. Then it was me, Corinne Hawkins, Debra Smith and Lanie Bright. We got 100 each. That kept us in groceries for two weeks, Scratch."

Scratch nodded. "It's OK, Immy. You don't have to explain yourself. Who was at the party?"

"Older, rich white men. I don't really know who they were by face. Except one was talking about owning a newspaper."

"Local paper?"

"Yeah..uh... Message?" Immy said.

"The Daily Message," Scratch said.

"At first it was just a card game. They were gambling over us girls. Over what kind of..." Immy looked away and cleared her throat. "What... kind of sex acts we would do to them. They were gambling over this hatbox. One old man got real pissed off when he didn't win. The newspaper owner won. Then it got real ugly, Scratch. There was this younger white guy serving drinks. We saw him sneak that hatbox out the trailer. He got in his car and drove off. Those old men started rantin' and ravin'. Throwing things at the car. No sooner did they kick us girls out, Colman Sheriff department showed up."

"Deputy Shaw, I figure," Scratch started to pace, and Immy stopped him.

"Don't, Allan," she said. "You're getting on my nerves."

"I need a cigarette. You have any?"

"I have a pack of Silks in my purse. I'll get them for you."

Silks were marketed to women. Supposedly not as strong as Winstons, won't hurt your throat like Virginia slims. All bullshit. A cigarette is a cigarette. If you're hooked, you are not worrying about taste as much, or making your throat raw. You want that tobacco to put you in the right frame of mind.

Immy returned with a black-and-white package. She handed it to Scratch gingerly, put her hand on top of his for a moment.

"Everything will be all right, Allan."

Scratch nodded, jerked his hand away. He took two cigarettes out, lit them both, and gave one to Immy. They smoked together in silence for a bit. Then he asked her to continue the story.

"Well," she said, "Shaw pulled us over. Shaw was happier than a pig in shit. Using all kinds of foul language, calling us jigaboo girls and such. Asking us what we were doing in white-man land. He answered his own question. Saying he knew about the party, he knew what was going on. He knew we were hired whores," Immy took a few drags before continuing. "He ordered us out of the car. He lined us up and had a free feel while he was frisking us. His hand lingered in some places longer than it should have. When he finished frisking me, he pulled his hands away like something bit him. He studied my face long and hard. It was weird. He let us go. He said he was real sorry for our trouble. He acted embarrassed, rushed to his car and sped off."

Scratch finished his cigarette and stubbed it out in an ashtray Immy kept on the mantle with all the family pictures. Scratch's eyes scanned every picture of him and Immy. His mother and father. He looked closer at the picture of Immy and their mother. Son of a bitch, he thought. Immy looks more and more like their mother. Cocoa-skinned, large brown eyes, long, straight black hair, full lips and high cheekbones. But Immy and their mother reminded him of somebody else. He couldn't quite put his finger on it.

"You think Shaw is blackmailing us?" Immy said. More of a statement than a question. She stubbed out her cigarette in the same ashtray, put a hand on her brother's shoulder.

"Yeah. I do," Scratch said. 'Just not sure who the woman is helping him."

Scratch kissed Immy on the cheek. "See you later, Sis." He headed for the front door.

"You're leaving? Don't you want to have breakfast with Micha and Justine?"

"I'd like to." Scratch opened the front door and stepped outside. A nice breeze was blowing. Thunder crashed in the distance. "But I can't, Immy. Going to see Dobro."

"Allan." Immy threw her hands on her hips in protest. Just like their mother used to. "Don't get caught up in Dobro's shit."

Scratch laughed. "More like he's getting caught up in our shit, Sis."

The door slammed behind him.

13

The '48 Dodge pulled into a dirt parking lot. Rain was coming down steady and lightning flashed in the dark sky. The Lock and Key club, a stucco building with one stained-glass window showing a faded image of Mary and Jesus holding hands, had been a Methodist church before WWI. Despite the hour, the club was still going strong. It wasn't just a place to hear the blues and get drunk. In the back was a room for gambling. Beside that room, a projector showed blue movies on the walls.

You could also go upstairs and get laid, too. Whatever you want. Black women, white women, Hispanic. One Asian woman worked there, but the other whores disliked her so much that one night they banded together and stoned her out of town. You can get you a sissy, if that's your game. Only they were in the minority in Dobro's stable. No judgement from the management as long as you followed house rules. No rough stuff, unless you pay extra and the whore is OK with it. No killing anyone inside the club, take it outside. Always be courteous to the cops.

Dobro managed the Lock and Key for Scratch's Uncle Homer. Uncle Homer had his hand in every business in Darktown and Pennywald, another segregated area 25 miles west of Odarko. Homer wasn't too different from Spiff. Just not as rich. Scratch was more than certain that was the goal for dear Uncle Homer.

Scratch walked in the door of the Lock and Key and found wall-to-wall people. A frail skinny black man with an electric guitar bigger than him stood on a small round stage just to the left of the bar. Multitudes of people, mostly women, surrounded the stage, swaying to the music, possession in their haunted eyes. The man howled and screeched, slid a beer bottle across the guitar strings. A fight broke out between two men in black suits and white panama hats.

A bottle was broken on one man's arms and he threw two jabs at the other man's chin. They wrestled toward Scratch, who promptly opened the door, stepped outside to let the men roll past him. Scratch came back in and closed the door. The club erupted in laughter and applause, hands clapping fiercely.

Scratch turned to each corner of the room and bowled. More people cheered, hooted at him. Scratch felt a hand on his shoulder. He looked up and saw it was Dobro. They gazed at each other and no words were spoken until Scratch leaned in and hugged Dobro.

"Brother," Scratch said.

Dobro laughed, hugged Scratch back. "Brother! Been too damn long!"

"I know, I know," Scratch said.

"Let's get a drink," Dobro pointed to a door with a sign stating keep out.

His office was under the staircase leading to the rooms the whores did their business and the theater where men paid a quarter to see films of people having sex.

"Wolfy! Going to my office!" Dobro yelled over top of loud chatter and driving guitar blues. A tall, bearded black man looked up. "Bring us a bottle of Tennessee!" Wolfy waved, and when he noticed Scratch, he laughed and pointed. Scratch smiled, pointed back. Wolfy came from behind the bar and handed two shot glasses to a woman in a red dress, said he'd see her in 10 minutes. She kissed Wolfy and turned to walk away, but was held up momentarily when Wolfy placed a hand up her dress. She laughed and wiggled more, looking over her shoulder at Wolfy.

Dobro unlocked the door to his office and flipped the light switch on. Nothing much to brag about. A desk, two chairs and a leather couch. The bookshelf behind the desk had lobby cards from all the movies Dobro had seen. Posters of Bogart and Mitchum plastered the walls. A framed autographed photo of Betty Grable sat on the desk with Cab Calloway and the Nicholas brothers.

"Have a seat," Dobro said. He sat behind his desk. He opened a drawer, removed two large glasses and set them on the desk. "What brings you back to Darktown, brother?"

"Thought I'd see you and Immy," Scratch said.

"How is your sister?"

"She's... OK." Scratch shrugged.

There was a knock on the door. Dobro said to come in and Wolfy appeared on the threshold. He ambled over, set the bottle down, put a hand on Scratch's shoulder.

"I'm glad to see you, Scratch," he said. Scratch patted Wolfy's hand and thanked him. "Took care of that business with Reverend Joe, boss."

"Good, good." Dobro opened the whiskey and poured it into the glasses. "Want a drink, Wolfy?"

Wolfy shook his head. "You know I don't drink booze these days, boss. Booze makes me mean."

"All right," Dobro chuckled and sipped from his glass. I know Jaunita is waiting for you. Ya'll use room three. It's cleanest."

Wolfy nodded and went out of the office, closing the door behind him.

"You didn't come here just to see us," Dobro said.

"No," Scratch said. "I didn't."

"You need my help," Dobro extended his hand, sipped from his glass.

"I do," Scratch said.

"Tell me what you need, Scratch. You know if I can help, I will. Drink up."

"I really don't want any." Scratch pushed the glass aside. "I need some of those pills you have."

Dobro scoffed. "Bennies?"

"Yeah, those," Scratch said.

"You sure about that, brother? When was the last time your head laid on a pillow?"

"I don't need sleep, Dobro," Scratch said. "I need those pills."

Dobro licked his lips. He opened another drawer, took out a black bottle with no label. He stared hard at Scratch, then tossed the bottle to him. Scratch caught it with one hand.

"You ought to play for the Dodgers," Dobro chuckled. "OK. Tell me a story."

"Got a problem with blackmail." Scratch took the top off and poured a handful of pills into the palm of his hand. He chucked the pills in his mouth. Dobro watched in awe.

"A client, or Spiff has the problem?"

Scratch shook his head as he chewed the pills. "Me and Immy."

"For what?" Dobro asked. He finished off the whiskey in his glass and started on Scratch's glass.

"What happened to our father," Scratch said.

"That was a long a time ago," Dobro said. "I don't even think anyone remembers that happening."

"Somebody does."

"You know who?"

Scratch took the letters from his jacket pocket and threw them toward Dobro. The papers fell on the empty glass. Dobro snatched the letters, eyeing Scratch. He read them in silence.

"Hmph! OK. You want five hundred from me? No sweat," Dobro said. "I'll borrow it from your uncle."

"Not paying," Scratch said.

"Oh?"

"Not paying."

"Then what?"

"I want you to help me get this blackmailer," Scratch said.

"You didn't say who it was. Somebody from Darktown?"

"Too white."

"Who is it, then? Shit, boy! Anybody teach you how to tell a story? You start at the beginning," Dobro put the bottle in the top drawer, slamming it shut. He leaned across the desk, pointed a finger. "You want me to help you make this blackmailer disappear."

"Yeah," Scratch nodded. His eyes became wild. He could feel the pills working, like a lamp plugged into an electrical outlet, electricity hitting every nerve in his body.

"Tell me who it is, then," Dobro ordered.

"Smell the paper," Scratch told him.

Dobro did. He pulled his head away quickly. "Damn it! Coulda told me it was lye!"

"The blackmailer was trying to remove a stamp or a seal already on the paper," Scratch said. "Look at the top right side. Hold it under a light."

Dobro removed the lamp shade on the lamp on his desk. He turned it on and held it to the paper. He laughed, sat the lamp back in place, and the shade back on it. He stared at Scratch and smiled.

"Coleman county Sheriff's department," Dobro said. "You're talking about wiping Rooster off the face of the earth and not thinking anyone would notice or care? Hell, your uncle has dealings with Rooster!"

"Not Rooster," Scratch said. "Deputy Shaw."

"That's another story." Dobro raised an eyebrow.

"He wants to meet at the lake at 10pm tomorrow night."

"Hmm…" Dobro thought about it. "What I can do is arrive with Wolfy much earlier from Darktown side."

"Don't bring Wolfy. I don't want anyone else knowing about this," Scratch said.

"OK." Dobro shrugged. "I'll just come early. You arrive a little after 10, the way he would come."

"Then what?" Scratch asked.

"That depends on Deputy Shaw and the choices he makes."

"Good answer," Scratch popped a few more Bennies.

"Slow down," Dobro laughed. "You'll do yourself a mischief."

"I can handle it," Scratch said.

"You sure you can?" The old Korean man said. He was standing over Scratch, holding a stick high above, ready to strike Scratch across the shoulders.

Scratch fell backwards. Both he and the chair spilled over.

Dobro jumped up from behind his desk and rushed to Scratch's aide.

"What the hell?" Dobro screamed. "Are you all right?" Dobro offered a hand.

Scratch nodded and took his hand. He used Dobro to hoist himself to his feet. Two gunshots sounded. There was a hubbub of raised voices as panic filled the Lock and Key. The door opened quickly. Wolfy poked his head in.

"We got troubles, boss!"

"No shit! I can hear the commotion, Wolfy," Dobro said. "C'mon, brother," he said to Scratch. "Might need you to do your specialty."

"You have Wolfy," Scratch said.

"Naw," Dobro chuckled. "He breaks heads. He can't get inside 'em like you do, Mr Scratch."

People were running out the entrance and exit in droves. Screaming, waving their hands, pushing, and trampling each other. Wolfy led the way down the hallway, pushing onlookers and hangers-on to the side. Most of them were johns trying get their clothes on or whores trying to keep themselves safe.

A light-skinned black man in a black suit was on his knees, praying. A Colt .45 Cavalry issue lay beside him, the barrel of the gun smoking. He had two scars across his bottom lip. Chester Goode was his name and he'd served in World War II in the Pacific. Shrapnel had sliced Chester's lips not once but twice, which affected the way he spoke. But Chester had money, working at the chicken factory. He never spent it and he lived with his mother until she passed two years ago. Celeste Holmes took an interest in the introvert, shy man.

She was lying dead in her bed as was the milkman, Tyrone Radford. Celeste was naked except for black stockings. There was a bullet hole as big as Texas was between her breasts. Tyrone's face was practically obliterated.

"Sweet Jesus," Dobro murmured and looked away.

Even though Dobro was a pimp and thought he was a hard man, seeing dead bodies, especially people he knew, disturbed him. Scratch placed a hand on Dobro's shoulder.

Chester finished praying. He reached for the .45 and Scratch screamed, "No!" and tackled the man. Dobro kicked the gun out of the way as Scratch pinned Chester to the floor. The man started wailing, screeching like a barn owl. Scratch struggled to hold Chester, rolling on the floor, tearing Chester's suit until he gave up. Chester sobbed hard. Once in a while he would call out for his mother.

"Let me gooooooooooooo!" Chester screamed. "I did what any man would do! You know that! You know that!"

Cowboy boots entered the room, spurs rattling with every step. Long, pointed brown tips were almost touching Scratch's face. Scratch looked up and saw it was Culky Lowe. He looked even taller in his wide-brimmed Akubra. His milky-brown skin had started to peel around his cheekbones, giving his pale blue eyes a haunted look. Culky stood there, his hands on his fat belt, a .32 Smith and Wesson stuffed near the oversized belt buckle.

A little history on Culky Lowe.

Culky had been a cowboy all his life. He was a veteran of World War II. Long before that, at the age of 10, Culky got his first job on the trail. First with sheep farmers, then running steers to Chicago. He worked his way up to trail boss with Douglas Northup, one of three men who supplied beef to the west coast.

Tired of taking orders, Culky found himself in Darktown, owning a ranch just outside the town border. He had a Cherokee wife and one daughter. Susan grew up, moved to New York City and died of chickenpox. The Cherokee wife left Culky soon after. Culky hired Saul and Hoke a year or so after. Five years later, a bank robbery happened. No one knew what to do. No one had ever attempted to rob a bank in Darktown, and the bank was owned by Scratch's uncle. There was going to be hell to pay. Culky and his men saddled up and found the two men. He brought them to the town square and strung them up. Ever since, Culky Lowe had been the self-professed Sheriff of Darktown, keeping law and order.

Culky chewed rapidly and spat tobacco juice on the floor. Two other men appeared behind him. Saul and Hoke. They would be Culky's deputies, if any of the three had been real men of the law.

"Seems like every time you come back to Darktown you cause a ruckus, Scratch Williams," Culky said.

"If that was even true," Scratch said. "You and your boys would be busier than sitting on your porch whistlin' Dixie."

"Let him go, Scratch," Culky said through a flared nostril. "We got it from here."

Scratch removed his hands from Chester's arms, which he had pinned to the floor. Scratch stood, straightened his hat and wiped dust and dirt from his jacket and pants.

"You seem to show up at the right time, Culky," Scratch said.

Culky sneered. "You seem to show up at the wrong time, Mr Scratch."

They glared at each other. No love lost there. Culky had always hated Scratch. Some sort of jealousy? Or the fact that he could travel between two different societies? The latter was the more likely.

"What happens to Chester?" Dobro asked.

Culky shifted his eyes to Dobro. "You know what happens."

"Come on, Culky. Everybody knows Chester ain't all there."

"He's gotta pay," Culky said. "Justice has to be served here in Dark-town."

"To keep everybody in line?" Dobro said.

"You don't have to do this, Culky," Scratch said.

Culky turned quickly to Scratch. "Uh-huh. I don't, but I'm going to."

"There's another way..."

"You think this is Odarko?" Culky cut Scratch off. "This ain't your white boss's territory, Mr Scratch! He don't own Darktown! Oliver Spiff only has his big toe on our soil and it's because of you and your uncle. That's all."

"I'm not going to let you do this..."

The butt of Saul's .38 caught the back of Scratch's head. Scratch fell immediately. He hit the floor with a groan. Saul pointed his .38 at Dobro. Dobro held up his hands and backed away. Hoke and Culky led Chester out the room, but before they left, Culky had one more thing to say.

"I keep telling your boy," he said to Dobro. "He don't have nothin' to do with Darktown. Get his ass out of here!"

Chester screamed, wailed, and bawled all the way to the town square. He mumbled prayers, apologized to his mother, and cursed the devil for making him kill his woman and the man she was cheating with. In reality, Celeste was a prostitute and the murdered man was just a traveling salesman, his first time at a house of ill repute.

Scratch gathered himself and he and Dobro trotted after Culky and his men to stop them. When they got to the town square, Culky already started the proceedings and everyone who had been in the club gathered around folks who woke up and came out of their houses to see the ruckus.

"It don't matter what color you are," Culky said to all witnesses. "Whether you're a man, a woman... God expects you to act in a certain way in polite society. He don't want us to run around..." He looked at a weeping Chester, who kept falling to his knees and at Saul, who kept picking him up. "...killing each other."

A rope was tossed around the post office sign. It had been pre-tied into a noose at the end. So it was true. Culky drove around with nooses in his trunk looking for an execution. The noose swung as Hoke tied it around the sign. Saul grabbed Chester by his collar and made him stand, but Chester kept falling to his knees, unable to stop sobbing, apologizing to God and his mother.

Saul reached for him again and Culky shook his head. Saul took a few steps back, and Culky stepped forward.

"Aw hell," Culky said. "You're a waste of good rope, any damn ways!"

Culky took his .45 from his belt and shot Chester twice on the left side of the temple. Chester fell to the side in a pool of his own blood and brain tissue. There was a gasp from the crowd. A long silence fell on the night. Even the night creatures were silent, horrified by what they'd witnessed.

Several houses down, Scratch saw the young black man who had vacated his car a few hours before. He was standing outside a white shack with moss growing on the roof. He was in a black T-shirt and underwear. An elderly woman came out, looked at what happened, then ushered him inside. Before he closed the door, Dobro got a good look at the man.

"Dobro." Scratch pointed. "You know him?"

Dobro snickered. "Oh, yeah. Felix Crump. That's the twist that shot at you?"

"Yep," Scratch answered.

"Hmm. Well," Dobro started to walk. "Let's talk to him."

Scratch put a hand on his arm. "No." Scratch shook his head. "We go over there, he sees us, Dobro, and that punk will turn and run. I need to watch him."

"Maybe so, yeah," Dobro said.

"I'm betting that's his grandmother," Scratch said.

"Unless he's doing old ladies again."

"Do what?" Scratch was shocked.

"Boy was hustlin' old ladies a year or so ago. Get 'em to feel sorry for his ass, take him in. Live in their house for a week or so, then take off with money, jewelry… Fucker moved on to guys. That shit didn't work too well. He got his ass beat too many times."

"Damn," Scratch said in disgust. "You manage him?"

"Hell naw!" Dobro was offended by the question. "I don't manage trash like that. Even my sissies are prime! You know that, Scratch."

Scratch smiled, put a hand on Dobro's shoulder to let him know he did know that.

"Now I know where his base of operations is," Scratch said.

"What? Now you pullin' some army shit out," Dobro laughed. "Come to my place, brother. Tina will fix us some steaks and greens. Get you some much-needed shuteye before your big meeting."

"Thanks, Dobro, but no thanks. I'm going to watch Felix."

"Suit yourself," Dobro said. 'Tina's gonna be sick she ain't seen you."

Tina was Dobro's common-law wife. They had four kids together. All under 12. Tina liked men as much as Dobro liked women. Both jealous as all get out, both crazy as hell, nearly killing each other more than once. Both still together. Both needed to be a thousand miles away from each other.

'I'll pop in and say hi when all this is over with."

Dobro knew better. His brother wasn't going to see Tina, not after the blowout last year when Scratch caught her messing with one of the oil rig workers. She messed that poor man's head up. Ruined his marriage. The wife left, took the kids, and the oil rig worker killed himself in front of Scratch. Shotgun to the face.

"OK, brother." Dobro walked away. "You know where to find me."

14

Nothing happened the rest of the night. Scratch sat in his Dodge, watching the house Felix lived in. At around six am, a light in the living room came on. A yellow hue glowed behind a thin white curtain. A short skinny shadow appeared. The curtain moved and an enlarged eyeball briefly appeared.

Way out in the distance, Marty Robbins's *Singin' the Blues* echoed. A few seconds, the music grew louder as a red Plymouth Fury roared down the cul-de-sac and came to a screeching halt at Felix's house. The same red Fury that had been driving around when the Klan was chasing Felix. The curtain moved again. Thirty seconds later, the front door to the shack opened up and Felix ran out, slamming the door behind him. He jumped in the car and it sped away.

Scratch started the Dodge and sped off behind the Fury. Two Cadillacs, one brown, one white, came out of nowhere and blocked the Dodge. Scratch hit the brakes, the car and he jerked forward, stopped just a hair from colliding with the brown Cadillac. Scratch smacked the steering wheel, watched the Fury drive off into the rising sun, Marty Robbins's voice echoing.

Two lean black men in zoot suits got out of the brown Cadillac and a six-foot-eight, 300-pound white man with a jigsaw scar that ran from the left side of his face to the right side, stepped out of the white Cadillac. The three of them hurried to the Dodge, opened the door and dragged Scratch out. Scratch belted the lighter-skinned black man, the darker-skinned one drove a punch hard into Scratch's midsection. Scratch fell to his knees, wheezing.

Pita-Paul was the big white guy's name. The underlings didn't have names. They were replaced almost weekly, either by haphazard deaths or jail. Pita-Paul had been Uncle Homer's bodyguard since World War II ended. A refugee along with his mother and a very beautiful red-haired sister called Heilke, they came to Darktown by accident, thinking they were in California. They ran out of money and the bus dropped them off thinking it was a funny joke to put Germans in the black part of Odarko, Oklahoma. The joke was on the bus driver. Uncle Homer offered the man a job right away. In spite of his lack of English, Pita-Paul and Uncle Homer understood each other from the jump. Mama and Heilke also lived in Homer's house, the only mansion in Darktown and almost as big besides Oliver Spiff's. As anyone could guess, Heilke was Homer's third wife, and his prized possession. The main wife, Delilah, lived in the big black house on Hubbard with the two boys, just before the line into Odarko, while the second wife, Alma, lived alone in a yellow shack not 100 yards from the chicken factory.

It was Dozen Grant who stepped out of the white Cadillac, not Uncle Homer. Dozen was called that for two reasons. 1: He was the 12th and last child of Mimi and Garret Morris. 2: He was just an inch from being considered a dwarf. He had the features and his arms that were the same as those of a normal-sized man. The white suit he wore had to be specially made by a tailor in Tulsa, but the fedora was bought from a five-and-dime with money from his first bank job, which turned out to be his last. Dozen spent five years on a state farm before he broke from a chain gang and had been a wanted man for the last 15 years.

Dozen got out of the white Cadillac and scuttled over to Scratch and the others as quickly as his little legs could carry him. The lighter-skinned black man kneed Scratch in the face.

"Whoa!" Dozen called out. "Hey stop, you fools!" By the time he'd gotten over there, the two zoot suits had roughed Scratch up some more. "The hell are you two doin'?"

"Doin' what you said, boss," the darker-skinned one said.

"Yeah... you said..."

"I ain't said no such thing, you dumb motherfuckers! You think I would tell you rough up my employer's fuckin' nephew?"

"What?" The lighter skinned man was stunned. His nose wrinkled in disgust.

"You tellin' me this white jack-off..."

"He ain't all the way white, you dumb assholes!" Dozen sighed. He touched the bridge of his nose and closed his eyes for a moment, trying to calm down a raging migraine.

"You said to rough up the white guy..."

"Stop talking, please. Damn it to hell! You were supposed to stop the red Fury, you lamebrain," Dozen said. He walked over to Scratch and helped him to his feet. "Man, I'm sorry, Scratch."

"That's OK, Dozen," Scratch said, breathless. He stood, woozy, and steadied himself by leaning on the little man.

"You fools bring Scratch to the white Cadillac."

"I ride in that!" The lighter-skinned guy said.

"You ride in the brown Caddy or you fuckin' walk!" Dozen said.

The zoot suits didn't like what they were told, but were powerless to do anything about it. They helped Scratch inside the white Cadillac. Zeke was driving. At one time Zeke hung out with Scratch and Dobro, until he and Dobro had a fight over a girl. He let those zoot suits beat up on Scratch because of that. Scratch was sure of it.

"Scratch, my man. How's it going?" Zeke asked with a laugh.

"All peaches and cream, Zeke," Scratch mumbled.

"Zeke, shut the hell up and drive!" Dozen slammed the car door.

"Yes, sir." Zeke continued to laugh as he put the Cadillac in gear.

15

Uncle Homer was sitting by the fireplace, lost in thought. He was still in his silk tiger-print pajamas. Heilke was on the sofa in her slip, sliding a stocking on to her right leg. A dead black man laid on the floor. His trousers were round his ankles and there were two gunshot wounds in his back.

Dozen pushed his way through everyone. He walked around the room, surveying the situation. Dozen threw his hands up in the air. "What the hell happened? Why is Delmont dead?"

Without looking at Dozen, Uncle Homer said: "Babycakes was fuckin' this guy."

"And?" Dozen said sarcastically. "She fucks a lot of your guys, boss! It's what she does! You know this, you approve."

"Naw, Dozen," Uncle Homer shook his head slowly. "This is different."

"Well? Explain," Dozen said, placed his hands on his hips and bounced his head up and down like an angry hen.

"He was planning to cut me," Uncle Homer said. There was a sadness in his voice. Disappointment. "You never expect your own people to try and take you out like that. I've known Delmont since he was three years old. His daddy used to work in a rock quarry with my cousins. I took Delmont under my wing. You never expect your own people to gather around and rip you apart – to feast on you. It didn't used to be that way."

"I'm trying to understand this," Dozen said. "Delmont was fucking Heilke?"

"Making love is natural!" Heilke said, as she slipped the other stocking over her left leg.

"Shut the hell up! Ain't nobody talking to you, little Miss Hun!"

Uncle Homer still didn't look at anyone. He raised his hand and waived dismissively at Dozen. "Dozen, don't, please. I'm hurting enough as it is. I don't need to witness you and Babycakes disliking each other."

Dozen noticed Uncle Homer had slipped into his other personality. He had many faces, all of them a left turn from the actual Homer, the real Homer, who was Boss of Darktown. The real Homer was the dangerous one. The one Dozen liked the most.

"Son of a bitch!" Dozen exclaimed. "The boss has got the blues! OK, OK. Everybody out! Get Delmont and put him in freezer until we can get Ferdie for a funeral."

"I don't have to leave," Heilke stood, stomped her feet. "I am his wife!" she said, her accent growing stronger. "I hate you all! Pig-fuckers!"

"Bitch, get the hell out of here and go to your damn room!" Dozen screamed and trotted to Heilke. She held out her hands, her long red fingernails ready to claw his skin off, take an eyeball out if need be. Pita-Paul stood between the two of them, sighing deeply. Dozen stopped short of running into Pita-Paul's thigh.

"Everyone leave!" Uncle Homer yelled.

The light-skinned black man grabbed Heilke by the arm and jerked her toward the door. She cursed and spat at everyone. Pita-Paul and the dark skinned black man picked up Delmont and carried him out the room. Dozen shrugged at Scratch and motioned for him to go out ahead of him.

"Wait. Scratch, you stay," Uncle Homer called out.

Dozen shrugged and turned to walk back in after Scratch.

"Just Scratch," Uncle Homer said with enough attitude that if anyone lit a match, the house would catch fire.

Dozen left the room, cursing under his breath. He slammed the door behind him.

Uncle Homer glared at Scratch, fuming.

"Where's your eye, boy?" he asked.

"I was at the right place at the wrong time," Scratch said. "Somebody jumped me. I think it fell out. They took it."

"Pokin' your nose where it don't belong again," Uncle Homer said. "You were in the right place at the wrong time because of your employer?"

"Why do you want to see me, Uncle Homer?"

"Scratch, I love you – you are my dead sister's son and I love Immy. But you two…" Uncle Homer laughed. "You two are a handful. I promised your mama I'd look out for you both." Homer pointed a finger at Scratch. "Look how you brats repay me! Working for the white devil! The one man who wants what I have!"

Homer produced the same .38 that killed his bodyguard Delmont. Anger rose up in Scratch. Not from having a gun aimed at him. Not because his own flesh and blood was thinking of killing him. But because the statement that he loved Scratch and Immy was a complete lie. So was promising their mother Uncle Homer would look out for them. Scratch wasn't deterred. He sat there stone faced. He wasn't going to feed into Homer's psychosis.

Homer laid the .38 on the arm of his chair. He laughed wildly.

"You *are* Mr Scratch," he said. "Nothing gets to you."

"Why do you say Spiff wants the one thing you have? He already has Odarko," Scratch said.

"Exactly," Uncle Homer said. "I have Darktown. Why would he want this piece of shit? He doesn't."

"You just said…"

"I didn't say he wants Darktown, boy! I said the one thing I have, he don't have!"

OK, Scratch thought. *Now he's not making any sense.*

"Why was Immy at that party?" Uncle Homer asked.

"You were there?"

Uncle Homer shook his head. "No. I don't need to go to that dumb shit. I have my own parties. One of my boys was there." Homer looked away. Sadness seemed to come over him. He lifted a slow, uneasy hand to his head. "I can't keep doing this, Allan."

That was the first time Uncle Homer had called Scratch by his real name.

"Do what, Uncle Homer?"

Homer sighed. "All this," he waved his hand wearily. "Y'all don't know what it's like to be the man. The one who has everything – the whole damn world sittin' on your shoulders. Spiff... Spiff knows. But he channels it a different way. He don't spread love – that mother-fucker is evil, I'm telling you, Allan."

Tears welled up in the man's wide, dark eyes. He sobbed for a moment, caught himself, and quickly found his composure, although his expression went through several personality changes.

But sad Homer won out.

"I want you to leave Spiff's employment," Homer said. "I'll groom you to have all this, Allan."

Scratch thought about it. He shook his head no.

"Thank you. But I can't anytime soon," he told Uncle Homer. "There's things I need to do before I can leave Spiff's company."

Homer snarled. He was fuming.

"Same old Mr Scratch, huh? Come to my house, bringing bad luck?"

"You sent for me," Scratch said.

"If you hadn't meddled, Delmont wouldn't have tried to kill me... and I wouldn't have killed him!" Homer stopped. Emotions were taking over again. Homer got choked up. He waited for the emotions to pass, and chose his words carefully. "I sent for you, for a reason, Mr Scratch. Funny... I was just tellin' Heilke about how your daddy tried to drown you in the sink because he believed you were the devil incarnate," he breathed in deeply, exhaled. "More and more I think about it," Homer grasped the .38 and aimed it at Scratch again. "That German motherfucker was right. You are the devil!" Homer screamed.

Homer went quiet. He fell forward in his mahogany chair and covered his face with both hands. It was quick, and the tender frail moment went faster than an Alfred Hitchcock whip pan. Homer straightened up, sniffled, and sighed. He glared at Scratch.

"Believe it or not, I love you boy." He shook his head and his lips curled up. "It's tough love. Not that bullshit love I give to my kids or Heilke. I let her do whatever she pleases, and look at the fucked-up shit I'm in." Homer laughed wildly, threw his hands up in the air. "Eh? You see it? You see the fucked up shit I'm in? You do. The more I think about this, Allan," he said, licking his lips, "the more I'm sure there ain't no heaven. There's only Earth..." Homer pointed to the floor. "And there's only hell. One and the same. The Bible is bullshit we made up to use for various reasons. Mostly for control."

"You still believe in voodoo and bad luck, though?" Scratch asked.

"I must," Homer laughed again. "You're still here."

Both of them fell silent, their eyes still locked on each other.

Homer pointed to a shelf with where a hatbox sat with a black stocking lying on top. Scratch stiffened.

"There it is," Uncle Homer said. "There's the hatbox your employer wants. Go ahead, boy. Take it. Ain't doin' me no good."

Scratch practically leaped out of his chair. He trotted over to shelf, pushed the black stocking off the hatbox. This was the hatbox in Ray Gardner's room. Scratch ran a finger across the gold initials, seductively across one S, then roughly across the other S.

"Were you at the party?"

"I already told you I was not at no party where George Spiff was at. However," Uncle Homer gave out a mischievous giggle. "I planned the event from my house. I gave strict orders to Ray Gardner to make sure Deputy Shaw would show up with photographer Betty Klein. She works for Horace Hammock. I didn't know Immy was going to be there."

Scratch cut his eyes at Uncle Homer.

"Do you know what these initials stand for?"

"I actually do, boy. Saundra Sommers."

"Wait… *the* Saundra Sommers?"

"Yeah. I told you. Saundra Sommers!" Uncle Homer yelled. "Take the fuckin' hatbox and get out of my sight!"

Scratch picked up the hatbox. It was very heavy.

"The hell is in this?" Scratch asked.

"Open it. See for yourself?"

Scratch sat the hatbox on the coffee table. He removed the top and found an 8mm camera inside, standing straight up. He looked at Uncle Homer.

Uncle Homer smiled. "There you go, boy. Now you see what Spiff wanted of mine and I didn't get what I wanted of his."

"That makes no sense," Scratch said.

"Hmmph! Coming from you? If you're confused, Mr Scratch, then the whole fucking world is doomed. Now get. Hey, Dozen?"

Dozen came running in, out of breath. "Yeah, boss?"

"Get him out of my sight before I shoot him!" Uncle Homer belted at the top of his lungs. His hand shook as he pointed the .38 at Scratch. His unsteady hand kept wavering between Dozen and Scratch. Feeling emotions getting ready to take over again, Homer turned, hid his face in the chair. His body convulsed as he sobbed hard.

Dozen led Scratch out of the room quickly. In the hallway, they stopped. Dozen tapped the hatbox.

"The hell you doin' with that?"

"He gave it to me," Scratch said.

"The boss gave that to you?"

"Yeah," Scratch said.

"That man is too damn crazy for me." Dozen touched the bridge of his nose. Another headache was coming on. "He told everybody: 'No matter what, don't let that shit-brickin' nephew of mine have that hatbox!' Damn, I can't take much more of this!"

"How long has he been like this?"

"Man, this has been going on for years. If you visited more you'd see it's often," Dozen said.

"I'm not as welcomed here as you'd think," Scratch said. "Bad luck."

Dozen sighed. "He does say that about you. He ain't never liked you or Immy. He liked your daddy, though."

"He did?"

"Hell yeah! Used him as a runner when the law was on everybody for having liquor. He found out your daddy was good with a car. Could get away from any cop..." Dozen laughed. "I guess he's still mad at you for the accident."

"Who else knows about the accident?"

"Not many people. Ain't many of us left from Homer's original gang," Dozen said. "Why?"

"Somebody knows what Immy and I did," Scratch said.

"That's surprising, since the story never hit the papers, never left Darktown. You need Homer to help?"

Scratch looked sour. He shrugged and shook his head. A thought entered his head, changed his expression.

"Can I have Delmont's body?"

"The hell do you want a dead body for?" Dozen asked.

"I got some use for him," Scratch answered.

Dozen scoffed. "Boy you are *weird*!" Dozen shook his head in disgust. "I don't know... maybe the boss is right. You might be the devil!"

16

Scratch drove out to Jesse Fulton's Diner on Route 10. He didn't expect to see Lilly in the place. But there she was. He started to run to her and kiss her long and hard but then thought better. He waited by the kitchen door to watch her, avoiding a waitress or two, who looked at Scratch as if he was some sort of creep.

Lilly looked at the clock behind the counter, got up from her table and started to leave. Scratch took three steps and called out to her.

"Lilly! Oh, hey! I made it!" He pretended to be out of breath.

At first, she didn't answer. She just happened to turn around and see Scratch.

"Ohh." she giggled nervously. "You are here!" Her eyes darted around the café.

Scratch's smile diminished.

"Who are you looking for?"

"Nobody," Lilly said. "Say, let's sit down, huh?"

Scratch reluctantly sat in a chair next to her. Lilly fidgeted with her skirt, held his hand in hers.

"Worried about something?"

"No." She was trying to act naturally. She laughed. "I'm surprised you're here."

"Exuberantly. Overwhelmed."

"I know what they mean." Lilly gritted her teeth.

"Who are you, really?"

"Ow! You're squeezing my hand..."

"Don't make me shoot you in front of everybody." Scratch squeezed harder and Lilly flinched, giving him a pleading look.

Scratch reached into the right pocket of his trenchcoat. He cocked the hammer of his .38. Lilly jumped slightly, gasping.

"My name is Betty – oww! owww!"

"Betty what?"

"Owww... Betty Klein! Please..."

"Photographer. You work for Horace Hammock."

"I work for a lot of people – I'm freelance. Owww, let go! I'll scream..."

"You scream and I'll shoot you dead," Scratch said. "That's a damn promise."

"Please, Allan..."

"Hold on... no one knows my real name. How do you know my first name?"

"Please let go."

"Tell me, now, Betty or I swear to God..."

"Deputy Shaw!" Betty squealed, her voice, loud enough to echo, interrupted the noise of the café. Scratch let go of her hand. All heads turned to look at them. A few minutes went by and everyone went back to their business.

"Is that who you're waiting for?"

"No," Betty said quietly. "I'm waiting for someone who can sell my pictures."

"OK. So, how do you know my real name?" Scratch asked.

A waitress came to the table.

"Everything OK, sweetie?" she asked Betty.

Betty smiled and nodded. "Oh, yes. Could we have some coffee? Want some coffee, honey?"

Scratch nodded. "Get us a couple slices of cherry pie, too," he told the waitress.

The waitress filled their cups and scooted back to the counter. She returned with two plates of cherry pie. She sat Betty's plate down easy but slammed down Scratch's plate. The waitress snarled at Scratch.

"Anything else?" she asked.

"No," Betty said. "Thank you."

"Of course, honey. You need anything else, just holler. Real loud." The waitress headed back to the kitchen.

"Go on," Scratch said. "Tell your story."

"I heard Shaw on the phone," Betty said. "I don't know who he was talking to on the phone, but he mentioned you, and the hatbox."

"By the way," Scratch took a bite of his pie, chewed it carefully and swallowed. "Where is the hatbox?"

"At my studio. You, uh, look in it?"

"No. I sure didn't. Is it money in it?"

"Uh, no. Kind of weird..."

"What-what are you doing here?" a voice demanded.

Scratch turned around and saw Harry Sanders standing behind him.

"Harry," Scratch chuckled. "Shouldn't you be at the drugstore?"

Harry sat down in a chair next to Betty. "I have a kid named Gary Palmer running it. Very nice, bright boy."

"Palmer? His brother is Hick Palmer?" Scratch asked.

"Yes. I believe so," Harry said.

"Interesting."

"That doesn't answer my question, Mr Williams."

"Now it's Mr Williams. What happened to calling me Scratch?"

"The company you keep has changed our relationship!" Harry sputtered, slammed his fist on the table.

Again, the whole café turned and looked at Scratch. He smiled at them. Harry tugged at his tie and his bottom lip quivered.

"I'm not sure who you're talking about, Harry. I've known you for two years and you've never acted like this..."

"You really are a son of a bitch. You know damn well what is going on." Harry's face turned bright red. He huffed and puffed while tiny beads of sweat rolled down his forehead.

"Harry, take it easy." Betty touched Harry's arm and he jerked away.

"Don't tell me what to do. I'm sorry, Betty. I'm very sorry." Harry tossed an envelope to her. "Here's the money. Where are the pictures?"

Betty opened her purse and retrieved her own envelope, only a little longer and fatter, green and bulky. She extended her hand and Scratch took the envelope from her. Harry lunged at Scratch. Scratch stood quickly, the chair fell from under him, making a loud crash when it hit the café floor. Harry saw the .38 aimed at him.

"I'll plug you, old man," Scratch said. "Come across that table again, and you'll be exchanging hellos with God."

Total silence in the café. Stunned faces, shocked, frightened eyes watched the scene unfold.

"Just… give the envelope back… please," Harry stammered, his bottom lip quivering. There was more to say but Harry's tongue, lips, and brain had everything twisted.

"I'm taking it and the contents inside," Scratch said. He placed the envelope in the breast pocket of his trench coat. He grabbed Betty by the arm and jerked her out of her chair. She squealed, trotted to Scratch against her will. She bumped him, and scratch threw his arm around her collarbone and neck. Betty dodged the .38 as it swung past her nose. "I'm taking her, too."

"I-I-I-I-I don't give a rat's ass about her!" Harry screamed. "I want those pictures!" His raspy voice blew out, hummed like a PA speaker with faulty wiring, and curdled the pitcher milk left on the counter by another patron.

Scratch backed away through a crowd of people. Women gasping, hands covering their mouths, men wanting to play the hero, except their nerves of steel had turned to mush. He pushed the door open with his foot and shoved Betty through the threshold. She yelped, stumbled outside, and fell on the sidewalk.

"You better find a way to get them back, Hoss," Scratch said. "Short of putting a bullet in my head!"

"That can be arranged!" Harry called out. "I don't care who you work for!"

Scratch let the door to the café close on its own then aimed the .38 at the bottom glass pane and fired into it. The glass shattered. There were screams and the crowd scattered. Scratch ran to Betty, picked her up by her blouse. The fabric on her sleeve ripped. Scratch practically dragged her to the Dodge. He motioned for her to get in, placed the .38 on her heaving breasts.

Betty smiled. She seemed to like the way he was treating her and that confused Scratch a little. She stepped toward him and tried to kiss him. Scratch turned from her.

"Get in the damn car!" he said.

Betty swallowed hard, gave him a lascivious look but dutifully did as she was told.

17

They were driving back to Odarko on Route 11. Neither said a word for a while until they approached the town limits. Betty was fidgety most of the ride. She would often turn to Scratch, sigh heavily, tut in frustration and shake her head. Scratch wouldn't look at her. He was thinking about his next move. Betty couldn't hold it in any longer.

"Say something," Betty said.

Scratch glanced at her.

"Oh. Come on." Betty rubbed her forehead. "I'm sorry I lied to you."

He wouldn't answer.

Betty rested her arm on the window frame and watched the trees pass by. "You could at least tell me where you're taking me."

"Going to your studio," Scratch said. Betty eyed him. "I have some film for you to develop."

Scratch reached over and placed his hand on Betty's knee. She put her hand on his. Betty smiled at Scratch and said: "OK."

* * *

"Pretty lewd photos," Scratch said, spreading out 20 glossy prints of women in various poses, some unclothed, touching themselves, others in lingerie or boudoir shots.

"They're just photographs to me," Betty said. She was finishing up developing the 8mm film in her bathtub, the film from the camera that had been in the hatbox. "I've photographed worse things. I'm telling you, Allan. Seeing a woman laid out on the blacktop without her head and her car smashed in like an accordion is 10 times worse than seeing her legs spread open."

"Not everyone agrees," Scratch said. He glanced at the bottom picture again. A brown-haired young woman in a see-through negligée and black stockings was lying on her back, cupping her naked right breast, pursing her lips. It was Maggi Spiff. "You know her?"

Betty adjusted her glasses, squinted. She smiled. "You like her, huh?" Scratch shrugged, pleaded with her to answer. "It's OK that you like her… Yeah," Betty chuckled. "She goes by Suzie Q. Dumb name, huh? She's very popular with buyers. Why?"

"She's actually Maggie Spiff."

"What? You mean… "

"Yep. Oliver Spiff's daughter," Scratch said.

Betty took a breath. "I didn't know, Allan. This guy met me in the Blue Room. We had a few drinks. He knew I was looking for girls to photograph. He said he had a guy, too. I never met the guy. He said he had three girls and a guy he tricks out, usually to rich businessmen. They'll do whatever they are asked to do. I told him I don't photograph anything the models are not comfortable with."

"Who's the guy?"

"I don't know his name. Harry set us up." Betty went on to describe the man. "He was short, portly, kind of muscled. He had a tattoo of a woman in dress sitting on an atom bomb. Kind of scary, intense – for a little guy."

Scratch chuckled. "Rudy Gilmore."

"You know him?" Betty asked.

"We've had a few run-ins," Scratch said. A thought came him. "Betty?"

"Yes?"

"Where's the other hatbox? The one you left Horace Hammock's house with?"

"I don't know, Allan," She sat on the toilet. "I was going to my car and a red Fury pulled up. This young man and woman were in the car.

The man got out and showed me a .45. He said he wanted the hatbox, nothing else. Of course, I handed it over."

"Did you look inside the hatbox?" Scratch asked.

"No," Betty said. She laughed. "I thought there was money in it. That's why I left with it. I thought I could use it to help with my mother's hospital bills. She has cancer." The thought of all those bills mounting up overwhelmed Betty. She had to focus. She wanted to help Scratch. "Why does everyone want that hatbox?"

"Two different camps with two different goals, Betty," Scratch said. "Two different bosses pulling the strings."

Some of the film started to come though. Betty tapped Scratch on the arm. She pointed to Images of three people becoming visible.

"Well," Betty laughed. "Looky, looky at the dirty pictures."

A woman was bent over on a canopy bed, her face buried between another woman's legs. A man was directly behind the first woman, entering her with his erect penis. The next 23 frames appeared after that, showing the man bucking hard and the second woman holding the first woman's bobbing head. The second woman looks at the camera, cups her right breast and smiles.

At that point, no other images came through. Betty drew Scratch's attention away from the negative. She kissed Scratch. He kissed her back, and she sat down on the toilet seat again. Scratch found himself on his knees, feeling the hard tile floor on his aching kneecaps. He kissed Betty's neck, moved to her collar bone, and finally to the naked right breast she'd just freed from her brassiere and blouse.

They would have done more but Scratch remembered two things he had not done yet. One: Go back to the Primrose and look at Gardner's room. The second thing was visit the offices of The Daily Message, the newspaper Horace Hammock owned.

"The film has to dry anyway," Betty said, placing the long black loops across a wire rack invented for undergarments to dry on. "I'll come with you."

Scratch hugged Betty from behind, caressed her breasts and kissed her left earlobe. Betty giggled.

18

Jerzy was hunched over his desk, reading the guest ledger. When he saw Scratch and Betty saunter through the lobby of the Primrose, he dropped his pen and straightened up as if an army sergeant had barked an order. He came from around the desk, and stared. Then he rushed to greet them.

"Mr Williams... uh... Scratch, my friend! How-how good to see you!" Jerzy's whole body shook, causing him to have a slight hiccup when he spoke. "Miss Klein... What brings you here?"

Scratch glanced at Betty.

"I took some family portraits and Christmas photos for him," Betty said.

"You celebrate Christmas, Jerzy?"

"Of course," Jerzy chuckled. "I'm an American now! I celebrate every holiday."

"Oh, yeah," Scratch looked at him incredulously. "Hey Jerzy, we're here to see the room."

"Room?" Jerzy smiled.

"Yeah, the room," Scratch repeated, smiling.

"You can check into 233. I believe that is free..."

"No, Jerzy," Scratch said. "The room where..." Scratch lowered his voice as a woman walked by and a bellboy followed, struggling with her suitcases. "The room where Ray Gardner was killed?"

Jerzy's eyes slowly eased down to his shoes. He swallowed hard. "I'm sorry, Scratch. That room." His eyes rose up again to meet Scratch's. "That room… is under renovations."

"What the hell are you talking about, Jerzy?"

"I was told to…"

"It hasn't been long enough for the police to gather all the evidence they need," Betty said.

"The sheriff know about this?"

"I-I don't know." Jerzy crooked his finger for Betty and Scratch to follow him. They went to the lobby desk. He removed some papers and revealed a cashier's check for 500 dollars, signed by Oliver Spiff. "I assume Shep knows."

"I'm going to call Shep, find out," Scratch said. He took a step and Jerzy caught the sleeve of his trenchcoat. Scratch stopped. Infuriated, he pulled away, but Jerzy held on.

"Mr Scratch," Jerzy shook his head, offered his closed hand. Jerzy motioned for him to open his hand. Reluctantly Scratch extended his hand and Jerzy dropped a ring in his palm.

"Where did you find this?"

Jerzy placed a finger over his lips, warning Scratch to keep his voice down. Then he pointed to the large man sitting in a chair too small for him. The man lowered the newspaper and turned the page. Pita-Paul was reading the comics page. His barrel chest occasionally heaved and a wheezing, screeching sound that resembled laughter of some kind came from somewhere among his three chins.

"What the hell is Pita-Paul doing here?" Scratch said.

Betty stifled a laugh. "That's his name?"

"Name he was given because the little bit of English he knows, every other word sounds like Pita-Paul."

"Mr Kurtzhun," Jerzy said.

"What?" Scratch quickly turned to Jerzy.

"My teacher," Jerzy said in a more broken-English accent than usual. "It pays to learn early in your life. In my school, Mr Kurtzhun, my teacher, you see, he tutored my brother and me in English."

Betty and Scratch looked at Jerzy sideways.

"He was a very good teacher," Scratch said.

Betty again stifled a laugh, placing her hand over her mouth.

Scratch turned the ring over in his hand, examining it. He leaned in and lowered his voice. "Where did you find this, Jerzy?"

"That night the state police came into your friend's room."

"Gardner?"

"Yes."

"Not really my friend, Jerzy," Scratch said.

Jerzy shrugged. "You tell me that."

"A little white lie," Scratch said.

"No color for lies," Jerzy wagged a finger. "Or size, Mr Scratch. A lie is a lie."

"Thank you for letting me know, Mother," Scratch said, and Betty burst into laughter.

"I don't care you lie to me. Friends do that sometimes," Jerzy said.

"Go on with your story, Jerzy," Betty said.

"The secret police—"

"The state police," Scratch corrected Jerzy.

"Yes. Them, too. They screamed. They pushed me. Waved their hands. 'Get out!' I show them. I call someone I know. I know well. I call Quincy Adams."

"You know the Governor of Oklahoma?" Betty asked.

"Yes," Jerzy's voice rose up an octave and he used his hands to show how much he disliked the question. "Why does everyone doubt me? He has stayed here at the Primrose. He and a young lady he adores very much."

"When was the last time he was here?" Scratch asked.

"The evening Mr Gardner was killed," Jerzy said.

Scratch sighed.

"What's wrong?" Betty asked.

"We have another player entering the game," Scratch said.

"Looks like your friend is leaving," Betty said.

"I think we're going to have to follow him," Scratch said.

"Mr Scratch," Jerzy placed a hand on Scratch's shoulder. "Please... be careful. I do not have a good feeling about that man."

They watched Pita-Paul march out the double doors of the Primrose and step on to the sidewalk. He looked left, then right, and threw both bulky hands on his hips. He looked antsy. This made Scratch even more curious. He took two steps to the right and plopped down on a bench.

"I think I'll be all right, Jerzy," Scratch said. "Betty will protect me."

19

A 1947 plum-red art-deco truck pulled up. The Chevy sat for a minute and the engine backfired a few times. The idle sounded rough. Pita-Paul didn't see the truck at first. The driver blew the horn. Pita-Paul waddled to the truck, opened the door and jumped in. The truck sped off before Pita-Paul could shut the door.

Scratch took Betty by the hand and they trotted to the double doors. Betty yelped and giggled as he pulled her behind him. She held down her skirt with one hand and kept her balance by holding the door frame with other.

"See you later, Jerzy!" Scratch yelled out.

"Be careful, Mr Scratch – oh, why bother? He's not going to listen," Jerzy said.

They rushed to Scratch's Dodge and hopped in. Scratch started the engine and sped off. A few blocks down the street, they caught up to the truck at a stop light. The Chevy pulled out easily when the light turned green. Scratch followed as the truck turned on Blueberry Drive.

They hit another stop light. A short, muscled arm hung out the window. On the forearm was a tattoo of a woman in a short dress riding an Atom bomb. Betty touched Scratch's leg. He glanced at her and she pointed to the arm hanging out the window.

"Rudy Gilmore," she said.

"I see," Scratch said. "We're going to have to see where these two end up."

"I think I already know," Betty said. "The Blue Room is right down the road."

"Is that a fact?"

"I have an idea, Allan," Betty said.

She reached into the pocket of her skirt and took out a tube of red lipstick. Betty leaned forward to see herself in the rearview mirror. Scratch smiled and watched Betty carefully apply the lipstick heavily, especially on her top lip to make them look fuller. She reached around and loosened the pink scarf from her ponytail. Her blonde locks fell on her shoulders. Betty pushed the strands around playfully, giggled, and removed her glasses.

She looked completely different. She no longer had the schoolteacher/secretary look. Now she was the bombshell every man dreamt of. Scratch couldn't keep his eyes off her.

"I think you better keep your eyes on the road, buddy," Betty said, laughing.

"Who knew this other girl was buried inside you,?" Scratch said.

Betty shrugged. "She comes out every once in a while for the right guy."

Inside the Blue Room, 12 people were sitting at tiny round tables with plastic pineapples obscuring their faces. Of those people, 10 were male, two were women, more than likely working girls, both talking to soldiers. Two men wearing Hawaiian shirts sat at the bar. They obviously worked at the Blue Room because, once Betty and Scratch entered, the two men went back to work, one behind the counter, while the other returned to the kitchen. The jukebox was playing *The Green Door* by Jim Lowe.

In the back of the room sat Gilmore. All by his lonesome self, nursing a glass of beer. On his right leg was a cast. Scratch found that very funny. So, Scratch thought, Gilmore was the Klansman I hit with my car. That makes sense. Gilmore kept looking around nervously.

Betty and Scratch sat at the bar. The bartender asked if he could help them and Betty spoke up first.

"Rum and Coke," she said.

The bartender did a double-take, and smiled at her. "I almost didn't recognize you," he said. "Then you ordered rum and Coke. New look?"

Betty was embarrassed. She smiled uneasily, fluttering her eyes. "Maybe. You like it?"

"Yeah," the bartender replied with a laugh. "Looks good on you."

"Thanks." Betty giggled and glanced at Scratch, who was showing slight signs of jealousy.

"You going to ask me what I want?" Scratch asked.

"Oh." The bartender gave Scratch a sour look. "What'll you have?"

"Just a Coke."

"A Coke? That's all?" The bartender laughed. "You know we sell alcohol here, bud?"

Scratch removed the small plastic bottle from his trench coat pocket. Popped the top off, threw his head back and swallowed five pills. He chewed each pill carefully and, the more he chewed, the wider, the crazier, his eyes got.

"Do you really think I should drink alcohol with these?" Scratch asked and laughed manically.

The bartender swallowed hard. Distress crossed his face. His eyes switched back and forth between Betty and Scratch.

"Yeah." the bartender nodded. "I'll get that Coke and rum and Coke."

"Are you OK?" Betty asked.

"I wasn't," Scratch said. His wild, frantic eyes met hers. "Now I am."

The bartender brought the drinks. He waited for payment. Scratch glared at the man.

"These are free." Scratch was telling the bartender, not asking.

Took a second for it to register, but the bartender went with it. "Oh." The man smiled, his jagged teeth looking like a child's drawing. "Sure, sure. Because I know Betty."

"You don't know her," Scratch said. "She wasn't in here today and I wasn't either. The drinks are free because you're a nice guy."

The bartender got even more nervous. "Yeah, yeah," he said. "That's right. Good to see you, Betty."

He left them to take care of a soldier standing at the end of the counter. The soldier ordered two beers and the bartender handed him two bottles of the Blue Ribbon.

"Go ahead and talk to Gilmore," Scratch ordered Betty.

"Allan, maybe we should wait..."

"I said go talk to him," Scratch said more forcefully.

Betty gave him a worried eye. She sighed and sashayed off.

The soldier started off for his table where another soldier was waiting on him.

"Hey," Scratch called to the soldier.

"What?" The soldier asked.

"Come here," Scratch smiled motioned with a hand.

"What do you want?" The soldier turned to Scratch. He waited for a smart comment, an insult, or an indecent proposal. He was tall and lean but with a barrel chest. His face seemed to be out of alignment, his ears didn't match, his left eye was higher than his right, and even his nostrils were disproportioned. It was as if he'd been drawn by the worst caricaturist ever to have picked up a pencil.

"Come on," Scratch said, laughing. "Have a seat, friend. Look, I want to ask a favor that will benefit you. Monetary."

"Speak English, mister," the soldier said. His attitude was exactly what Scratch hoped it would be. This guy needed some relief in one form or another. More than likely his friend came to the Blue Room to pay for female companionship or start a fight.

"I've 10 bucks for you and your friend to help me out with something," Scratch said.

"We ain't into weird shit," the soldier returned, angrily.

"Nothing like that." Scratch chuckled. He opened his wallet, threw a 20-dollar bill on the counter, followed by a five.

"OK, buster," the soldier shuffled over, sat the beers on the counter and took a stool beside Scratch. "I'll listen, then decide."

"All I'm asking is you open your ears, friend," Scratch said.

"I hardly recognize you," Gilmore said, grinning.

Betty giggled. "I am... sort of going through a bit of change."

"I like it," Gilmore said and they both chuckled. "Instead of taking those pictures, maybe you should get in front of the camera."

Betty giggled, waved a hand. "Oh, no. Not me," she shook her head. "I would be the worst model in the world."

"You wouldn't be modeling anything." Gilmore stared lecherously. He took Betty's hand in his, rubbed his thumb seductively across her fingers. "Just your body. Maybe we could go to your place and pretend – I'll be the cameraman and you be one of those models you photograph... "

"What do you think you're doing, Betty?" the soldier said.

She turned to him, then looked towards Scratch, who was hunched over at the bar, nursing a beer. He'd made sure his fedora was pulled down over his face.

"What?" Betty asked.

"The hell do you think you're doin'?" the soldier said. His buddy, a much larger, taller soldier, ambled over.

"Betty," the soldier's buddy said in a sorrowful voice. "Why do you do this to Joe? He's been good to you."

"I don't know either of you," Betty said.

"My parents are expecting us for dinner and you go out lookin' for company?" The soldier raised his voice.

Gilmore stood as best he could, the cast on his leg pulling him off balance. He placed two hands on the thin, flimsy table.

"You boys heard her," Gilmore said, sticking out his chest. "She said she doesn't know you. So if this some sort of gag, ha ha, the joke was told, nobody laughed. Shove off!"

"The only one shovin' off," the soldier said as he and his buddy moved closer to Gilmore, dwarfing him, "is your faggot ass."

"Is that the way they teach you fellas how to talk in the army?" Gilmore said, reaching in the right pocket of his jeans. "And in front of a lady, too!"

Betty knew a fight was about to happen. She got up and trotted to the bar where Scratch sat. Scratch smiled at her. Betty gave him worried glance.

Gilmore produced a small rubber club. He jabbed the fat end into the soldier, then came across the second soldier's face with it. The first soldier doubled over and coughed. Gilmore came back round to backhand the first soldier. Both were lying side by side weeping and moaning.

Scratch sighed. "Son of a bitch," he whispered.

Gilmore laughed. "Now," Gilmore said. "Before you two slime buckets crawl back in the gutter, apologize to the lady!"

A chair came across the back of Gilmore's neck. He cried out, fell on top of the soldiers, realized he was touching another man and panicked. He rolled to his left and discovered Scratch holding the chair.

"Damn," Scratch said. "It didn't break like in the movies," he marveled at the craftsmanship of the chair, switching from his left hand to his right hand, examining the seat and legs.

"Ahh! Why'd you hit me?" Gilmore whined.

The two soldiers helped each other up, and they hurried out the Blue Room as fast as their hurt bodies could carry them. Betty walked over to Scratch, watching Gilmore carefully. She touched Scratch's arm and he jerked slightly, realized he needed to turn his attention back to Gilmore.

Scratch tossed the chair down. He took the ring out of the breast pocket of his trench coat. He bent down and showed it to Gilmore. "This is yours," he said. "You set me up."

"The hell are you talking about?"

Scratch placed his shoe on Gilmore's crotch, applied some pressure. Gilmore screamed.

"You were at the Primrose the other day, in the room next to Gardner's," Scratch said.

Gilmore coughed, struggled to speak. "No I wasn't! I was nowhere around the Primrose!"

"You two run together," Scratch said.

"So what?" Gilmore said.

"This is your ring!"

"No, it's not!"

Scratch pushed his shoe in Gilmore's genitals, applied more pressure. Gilmore squealed.

"This is your Klansman ring!" Scratch bellowed.

"Noo, God, no! Look! Look!" Gilmore held up his right hand. A ring was on his first finger. A silver band with an engraved message preaching purity in the white race. A hooded figure stood in the silver stone with a red and yellow cross at the bottom.

Scratch looked at the ring in his hand. There was a cross on it, it looked nothing like Gilmore's. Scratch removed his shoe from Gilmore's crotch. "Hmm..." He said. "I was wrong."

Gilmore sat up. He coughed as he stood, using a chair for balance. "That ain't no Klansman ring, you idiot," he said, caught his breath. "That's a damn Nazi ring. Look at the stone. That's a swastika!"

Out of nowhere, a fist caught Scratch in the back of the head. The ring fell from his fingertips, bounced, then rolled across the floor. He heard Betty scream. Scratch wobbled, took a step and dropped to his knees. He raised his weary head, saw Pita-Paul standing over him.

The light went out in Scratch's head.

20

Scratch came to, and realized he was in the passenger seat side of his car. Betty was driving. The sun was going down and the cool wind from his car sailing down the highway had brought Scratch out of a forced sleep. He retrieved the Bennies from his coat pocket and popped the top.

"You sure you need more of those?" Betty asked.

"Don't tell me what I need," Scratch said.

"Look, I'm just concerned..."

"Don't tell me what to do!"

"OK, OK, Allan," Betty sighed. "Don't get upset."

"Stop calling me Allan," Scratch commanded, his voice severe, threatening.

"That's your name," Betty croaked. A nervousness came over her.

"Not anymore," Scratch said. "That's not who I am. I'm not Allan Williams, you hear me?"

"Yes," Betty replied after a long delay. She tried to touch his knee. Scratch jerked away.

"How do I know you're on my side?"

"I am," Betty said. "God, Allan – I mean Scratch – I am, truly, I am on your side."

"Where are we going?"

"Back to my house," Betty said. "The film is dry and..."

"I'm sick of this." Scratch stared out the window, watching the sky get darker. "I want to get away from all of this. Away from Odarko, Darktown, the hate... I'm sick of it. Sick of the lies. Sick of getting beat up. And for what? Some rich old ghoul who owns everything – and everyone. A ghoul who takes pleasure in everyone's misery. Why do I do it?"

"I-uh-don't know. Trying to make your world better, I suppose," Betty said.

"Fat chance of that," Scratch said. "My world is a disappointment. I was born just to make everyone miserable. Cause evil..."

"That's very harsh," Betty said.

"It's the damned truth," Scratch said. "The damned truth."

The Dodge came up on Betty's street. Black smoke and bright orange flames rose high above the horizon. Betty gasped. A fire truck passed them, nearly running them off the road. Betty stopped short of a ditch.

"There's a fire," she said.

Scratch sat up in the seat and looked beyond the first house. They were on a slight hill looking down. He shook his head, moved his eyes to Betty.

"Your house," he said.

"What?" Betty squealed.

"Yep." Scratch sat back down, popped a few more Bennies. The bottle was getting empty. He was more pissed off about that than Betty's house and the film burning up. He shoved the bottle in his coat pocket. "Your house is on fire. Now do you believe I spread evil?"

"How about we forget *you* for a moment and think of what *I'm* losing." Betty started to sob.

One thing Scratch couldn't stand to hear was a woman crying. Made him feel guilty when it wasn't his fault. This made him doubly guilty, since he felt all this was his fault. He threw his arms around Betty. She laid her head on his chest and wept quietly. *Thank God she's not a screamer,* Scratch thought. *I'd melt in her arms.*

When she was almost done, Scratch coaxed her to switch seats. He put the Dodge in gear and drove to her burning house. The firemen were working tirelessly to contain the blaze. Scratch and Betty stood with the other neighbors, watching the house crumble. Scratch moved his eyes to the onlookers' faces. He spotted someone familiar.

Dan Lowery was moving along quickly, looking behind him, trying to create a path through the crowd. An elderly woman tugged on Lowery's arm and he turned as if he was going to strike her. His expression changed and he plastered a fake smile on his face. He cordially greeted the old woman and spoke to her, even though his eyes were roaming nervously.

"Now what's Spiff's lawyer doing out here?" Scratch murmured to himself.

Felix was standing behind a huge tree, trying to conceal himself. He was taking a huge risk, a black man in the white part of town. Lucky for him, this neighborhood backed on to a wooded area that led into Darktown, albeit a six- or seven-mile walk. Still, if Felix got a good sprint on Scratch, he could hit the woods and not be caught. He had to be desperate to do that. Most of the firemen were in the Klan and if they spotted him, it was all over for Felix. They'd take him for a ride in the fire truck and he'd never be seen alive again.

"I have to dip out for a few minutes," Scratch whispered to Betty.

"Wait-why? My house is on fire," She tried to block him from leaving her side.

Scratch kissed Betty on the forehead. "I know, honey," He gently nudged her out of his way. "I think I see the person who did it."

"What?" Betty exclaimed. "Scratch! Get back here!"

Felix saw Scratch. He started to sprint but then Shep showed up. Felix tried to run to his left and Ralph appeared. He stopped and looked at everyone.

"I ain't do nothin'," Felix said calmly.

Shep put his hands out in front of him as he approached Felix slowly. "Take it easy, son. Nobody's gonna hurt you."

"I ain't do nothin'," Felix back-pedaled. "I aint do nothin'!" He screamed as he ran right into Ralph.

Ralph took him down immediately. That cowlick on Ralph's forehead twirled around and the long strand smacked him in the nose when he grabbed Felix by the arms and threw him violently to the ground. Ralph jammed his knee into Felix's back. He then rolled those wiry arms across Felix's back and handcuffed him. Ralph jerked Felix to a standing position.

"I ain't do nothin'!" Felix bellowed, sobbing hard. "I ain't do nothin' wrong!" Piss ran down Felix's pants leg and leaked on Ralph's left boot.

Ralph gasped. His dark, furry eyebrows arched down. "Son of a bitch! Those are new boots! I ought to bust your head in, boy!"

"Calm down, Ralph. The boy's scared," Shep said. "Put yourself in his shoes."

"I'd rather put him in my shoes so he could walk around in hundred-dollar custom-made boots with nigger piss on them!"

"I said stand down, Deputy!"

Ralph had never seen Shep angry. Scratch saw it once. At the Blue Room a year or so ago. An old adversary of Shep's had just finished a five-year sentence at Oklahoma state farm for armed bank robbery in Odarko. Words were exchanged, insults hurled at Shep's mother. Shep shot the man dead in the Blue Room. No one said a word, no one moved. Shep asked Scratch to help him throw the dead man in the swamp 60 miles away in a small Texas town whose name neither of them could pronounce.

No one was sad the man was dead and no one spoke of the incident. Ever.

Ralph thought of his future actions. He thought of what Shep might do. Ralph took a deep breath, and nodded to Shep. "Yes sir."

"Put him in the car, Ralph. I'll pay to have your boots cleaned," Shep said.

"Yes sir," Ralph walked to Felix to the police car, opened the door and eased him in the backseat, then slammed the door shut. He stood at the car with his back to Shep and Scratch, trying to get himself together and be less aggressive.

Shep turned to Scratch. "You OK? You look a little rattled?"

"I'm OK," Scratch said slowly.

"I've noticed something," Shep said.

"What's that?" Scratch rubbed his aching forehead.

"You don't like that word."

"What word?"

"Nigger," Shep replied with a grimace.

Scratch remembered when he and Immy were walking home from school one day in Oklahoma City. Some white boys gathered around them, throwing pebbles and taunting them. Saying: "Why are you walking with that nigger girl?"

He also remembered a neighbor boy who was sweet on Immy. They played together in that run-down building where they lived with a cousin for a short period. The boy's father forbade him ever to play with that "nigger girl".

Scratch never had any racial problems, unless Immy was with him.

"No," Scratch admitted. Their eyes locked. Burning embers in Scratch's pupils. "I've always hated that word. Hear it so much, it shouldn't bother me. But it does."

He wanted to confide in Shep. Tell him about his family history. But the trust level in Odarko, even between friends, was very low. If they knew anything about you, it came from rumor.

"I don't either," Shep lit a cigarette. "I'm hoping for change for his kind," Shep nodded toward Felix. "I don't anticipate any for the better. I hate to say."

Nothing else was said.

Shep finished his cigarette, tossed it on the ground and stamped it out. "We have a witness to the fire."

"You do?"

"Yeah. Old woman next door. She saw him," Shep nodded toward the police car. "Running away from the house on fire. I understand the woman you were with owns the house?"

"Yes," Scratch said. "Betty Klein. She's a photographer. Used to work for Horace's paper. She was in his house when I went to look around. We've partnered up some since."

"Is that so?" Shep asked with even more interest than before.

"We found a hatbox. It belonged to Gardner. A small film camera was inside it. I think he was making blue films. He may have even starred in some. Betty developed the film, but we didn't get to see much of it, just whatever developed on the negative."

"This case is all tangled up," Shep said. "I'm getting' too old to do Spiff's bidding."

"I have to tell you something," Scratch said. "Harry is involved with Gardner with pornography. The old man might be, too."

"The old man isn't involved," Shep said. "Not directly. Harry pays Spiff for protection. Just in case anyone tips off the Feds about his little pornography business. Harry thought he was protected by the Chicago mob. Spiff bought Harry from the mob."

"Maybe you should talk to Harry anyway," Scratch said.

"That will be difficult, Scratch."

"Why is that?"

"Harry is dead."

"Dead?"

"Yeah," Shep confirmed. "Shot to death in his drugstore."

"Robbery?"

"Yes and no," Shep sighed. He removed his trilby hat, ran a hand through the few strands of hair on his bald head, and placed the hat back on his head. "It was made to look like a robbery. Witnesses saw a Red Fury drive away. Before that Fury drove off, it stopped to pick someone up."

"Let me guess," Scratch said, pointed to the police car. "The car picked up Felix?"

"How'd you know?" Shep asked.

Scratch smiled. "I've had a run-in with that Fury, as well as Felix."

"That's his name, huh?"

"Yes. Felix Crump," Scratch said. "You mind if I talk to the woman who saw Felix burn Betty's house down?"

"I didn't say she saw Felix set the fire," Shep said. "She only saw him run away from the house. I don't mind at all. We work for the same man. As a matter of fact." Shep walked over to the police car. He leaned in the passenger's open window, spoke to Ralph. Ralph started the engine, put the car in gear and drove off, trailing a cloud of dust. Shep ambled back over to Scratch. "I want to talk to her again. Let's go."

"Mind if Betty comes along?"

Shep glared at Scratch.

"No," he said, his face contorted painfully in a moment of confusion. "I guess not. Was her house after all."

"Good." Scratch walked off. "I'll get her and we'll meet you over there."

21

Only one light was on in the whole house. A broken lamp with a dim light bulb that kept shorting out. The mood was weird and surreal. The house was cluttered with furniture stacked on top of each other, and pans and dishes hanging on the walls next to framed pictures with people's faces blacked out.

Betty let Shep enter the house first. She came behind him and Scratch brought up the rear. A large black roach crawled across Betty's shoe. She jumped, muffling a scream with her hand.

"Mrs Sommers?" Shep called out. No answer.

"Wait," Scratch whispered. He tapped Shep on the shoulder. "Saundra Sommers, the silent movie star?"

"Yeah," Shep said. "You didn't know she lived here?"

"No, I didn't."

"Been here for almost 15 years," Shep said. "Crazy as a bedbug. As you can see."

"How does a person get this way?" Betty asked.

"Family tragedies," Shep said. "On her way back from the east coast, in 1931, her husband was gunned down when their train stopped over here in Odarko."

"Train?" Scratch enquired. "I thought the only train running in this part of Oklahoma was in Presscott. We didn't get a train until 1934."

"Nope," Shep said. "That was the new train tracks Spiff and his father built. Much to our governor's chagrin."

"The governor opposed a train for voters?" Betty asked and sniggered. "How's he going to reach out to his constituents?"

"He's not and he doesn't need them," Shep said. "He buys the votes."

"Why didn't he want the train here? I don't understand," Betty said.

"He doesn't like anyone other than white people," Shep said.

"What's the story with Mrs Sommers?"

"They took my baby," a voice rattled from the darkness.

Her broken English sounded harsh to her new audience's ears. Betty even seemed to cringe at the old woman's voice – it was like something out of a Boris Karloff film. Old age had ravished a perfect speaking voice. Saundra Sommers had been a stage star in the early 1900s, in Berlin.

Saundra Sommers continued: "They killed my husband – shot him down like a dog. Took my child – drove off…"

"How many men? Do you remember what they looked like?"

"No faces. Just handkerchiefs, stockings covering their faces. I dream of those contorted faces every night. Ohhhh…" she cried out as if in sudden pain. "I'll never forget the size of one of them…" She paused. Perhaps recalling the memory of the man took time to dig into a vast bag of yesterdays. "He was a giant. The largest man I'd ever seen. He spoke fluent German."

Right away Scratch knew who she was talking about. Pita-Paul.

Mrs Sommers continued: "The one who shot my Konrad was a negro. He shot him like a dog. I had his blood all over me. I screamed and I couldn't stop. I've been screaming ever since."

Oh, now the timeline for Pita-Paul joining Uncle Homer was fudged. Or… Pita-Paul might have gone to Germany or been sent back. Homer took his family in when Pita-Paul returned.

"You paid the ransom," Scratch said.

"I keep paying it," Saundra said. "They never bring my baby back to me."

"Mrs Sommers," Shep butted in. "I need to ask you about the fire next door."

"Oh, God," she wept. "Hell is coming for all of us!" The old woman screamed and wept loudly. Betty went into the dark room. Shep and Scratch could hear Betty consoling Mrs Sommers.

When she calmed down, Betty whispered to her: "It's important that you answer the sheriff's questions about the fire. That was my house that burned down."

Shep waited to ask his question. Time for Scratch seemed to move the same pace as somebody drowning in quicksand.

"Mrs Sommers, did you see the negro boy set the fire?"

"No," she said. "I saw him run away."

"Did you see who set the fire?" Scratch asked.

"Yes." She started to weep again. Betty's voice was soft and serene as she tried to comfort her. Mrs Sommers controlled her sobs for just long enough to answer. "My nightmare was coming true. That fiend from hell – he set the fire, as I knew he would."

"What fiend?" Shep asked.

"The giant," Mrs Sommers said. "The giant burned that house down. He was coming for me! I know it!" Mrs Sommers became hysterical. Once again, Betty calmed her down. Told the woman to fix her mind on nice memories. Scratch doubted Mrs Sommers had any left. She started talking about the first time she met her Konrad. She kept talking, sometimes in broken English, other times in German.

They left Saundra Sommers talking to herself.

22

Scratch had to go back to Darktown. Betty didn't know why he couldn't stay with her and put his business off for a day. He tried to explain, but Betty didn't understand the situation because Scratch was cryptic about the details.

"Just trust me," he told her. "Please. Understand I have to take care of this and... I'll be at my place later."

"I don't want to understand," she said angrily. She looked away from his gaze and folded her arms.

"Get in the car," Scratch said. "I'll drop you off wherever you want."

"No, wait. Please, let me go with you."

Scratch thought about it. "I'm going to Darktown," he told Betty. "Are you sure you want to come with me?" He wasn't sure he wanted her to come with him. She'd learn more about him. She might even learn his secret. All Scratch could think about was how heavy that secret weighed on his shoulders. Maybe he should just let Shaw tell the world. Then he and Immy would have to answer for the killing of their father. All eyes on them, eyes on Immy for what their father had done to her, Scratch killing the man...

"I've been there before," Betty said.

"Oh? When?"

"Last year," she said. "Last Christmas. I took photos for the newswire. I'm not afraid."

"You went by yourself?" Scratch asked.

"No." Betty sighed. "Harry took me."

"Harry took you, but you were not taking Christmas photos of children unwrapping presents. Were you?"

"Yes! Yes, I did..." Betty fell silent. "And some racy photos of negro prostitutes."

"You sure you want to come along? I've got something to do. Betty. It won't be pleasant."

"I don't care," Betty kissed Scratch. "I just want to be with you. I'm scared, Scratch. I don't want to be alone. My house is gone. Most of my equipment... my work is burned up."

"OK," Scratch said. He popped a few more pills. Four were left in the bottle. He was feeling drowsy, and he could hear his own heart racing in his ears. He didn't want to go to sleep. He didn't want to dream about Korea, his father or anything, for that matter. "Wait in the car for me."

Betty kissed him again. This time Scratch didn't flinch. He accepted the long kiss passionately, even placed a hand under her skirt. He didn't care if anyone was watching. He had a knot in his stomach. A bad feeling this might be the last time he kissed Betty. She pulled away and removed his hand from under skirt.

"Later," she whispered and went to the '48 Dodge and slid into in the passenger seat.

Scratch looked in Shep's direction. Shep was enjoying a cigarette and trying not to watch Scratch and Betty. When he saw Scratch coming toward him, he turned away to watch the firemen working tirelessly to contain the fire.

"Shep," Scratch called out. "You riding with us?"

"Don't bother," he said. "I called Ralph from Mrs Stevens's house. He's coming to come get me."

"OK," Scratch said. "I'll swing by the jailhouse and talk to Felix in the morning."

"Oh, I almost forgot to tell you..." Shep finished his cigarette, tossed it in the street and stepped on it. "The old man summoned me today," Shep licked his dry lips. "I need a drink." He wiped his mouth.

"What did Spiff want?" Scratch asked.

"Me to keep an eye on you," Shep chuckled. "He's concerned you're going to Darktown too much."

"He wants me to get results doesn't he?" Scratch said.

"Well, yes. Of course." Shep chuckled again.

"Then he shouldn't care where I'm going," Scratch said.

"I think he's upset you haven't checked in," Shep said.

"Jesus, we just talked the other day!"

"You know how Spiff is," Shep sighed. "He's got to control every damn thing every damn minute. You don't how many phone a day calls I get. Sometimes... sometimes I wonder what our lives would be like if he wasn't around."

"Just another yo-yo controlling our every move," Scratch said.

"Yeah," Shep nodded. "I think you're right"

"I'll call him in the morning. Hey, I want to show you something," Scratch took out a piece of paper and showed it to Shep. "Have you seen any one wearing a ring with this in the stone?"

Shep looked at the paper closely. "Yes, actually I have." He examined the paper again. "Governor Adams."

"Quincy Adams? He wears a ring like this?"

"Scratch, if whatever you're mixed up in is involved with Adams and his people, drop it like a hot potato," Shep said. "Dangerous people. I'm telling you."

"What's the Governor of Oklahoma doing with a Nazi ring?"

Shep stared at Scratch. He sighed heavily. "WUNS."

"What the hell is that, Shep?"

"World Union of National Socialists," Shep said. He shook his head. "Damn Nazis. In America, Scratch. What's this world coming to?"

"I'm confused. You remember Pita-Paul?"

"Of course," Shep said. "He's a bodyguard for Homer Williams."

"He's been running around with Gilmore. He hit me and took the ring."

"Damn it, Scratch. I wish you'd come to me first," Shep put a hand on his right hip. It had been hurting him all day. "Where'd you get the ring?"

"Jerzy found it in the room Gardner was killed in," Scratch said.

"I think you know the answer, Scratch. Pita-Paul is not just working for Homer. He's working for the governor."

"Hold on." Scratch held up a hand. "If he's working for a governor who believes in white supremacy, then why is he a bodyguard for a negro criminal?"

"He's working for someone more powerful than either the governor or Homer," Shep said.

"Who could be more powerful than a governor?" Scratch asked.

Shep chuckled. "The people behind the elected official. That's who."

"The old man?" Scratch asked.

"George Spiff doesn't like Quincy Adams. I'm not sure what the reasons are but they dislike each other quite a bit. Maybe he's working against him."

"Was Pita-Paul kicked out of the country?"

"Yeah," Shep said. "Yeah, he was. Twice. Right before World War II started, and again last year."

"Why?"

Shep shrugged. "Old man Spiff called the Feds on him. I think it was a drug charge. I can't remember."

"The kidnapping of Saundra Sommers's baby," Scratch said. "Five men were involved. One a negro, we know that for sure. We also know Pita-Paul was the man Mrs Sommers described."

"We don't know that, Scratch!"

"Shep," Scratch reasoned, "how many six-foot-seven Germans do you know who live in Odarko?"

At that moment, Ralph came racing down the road, the police car fishtailing. He stopped just short of Scratch's shoes.

"Ralph, I told you not to be hot roddin' around with the police car!" Shep screamed.

Ralph stuck his out the window. Blood dripped from a gash on the right side of his forehead. "He's gone!" Ralph screamed back.

"What do you mean he's gone? What the hell happened to you?"

Ralph sputtered, tried to form the words correctly, but his tongue seemed to get in the way. After a time, he finally managed to spit it out. "Felix-the black boy. Somebody hit me from the side and turned Felix loose!"

Shep jumped into the police car and Ralph hit the gas. The car sped off, swerving, kicking up dust behind it.

23

The car ride to Darktown started out nice and easy, Cozy even, with Betty sitting very close to Scratch with his arm around her. No words were spoken. The closer they got to the other side, the stiffer Betty became. Scratch noticed she'd embedded her nails into her knee, going through her stockings, even drawing blood.

"Relax," he told her. "Everything will be fine."

Betty flashed an uneasy smile, removed her nails from her knee, and fixed her skirt so no one could see the self-inflicted wound.

They passed through an area of ramshackle houses and makeshift barns that were small grocery and butcher shops. Across from the church was a movie theater. Next to that was the school, a one-room building not much bigger than a shack. Betty took it all in.

They arrived at the lake.

A car was already parked and a man was standing at the dock, taking a piss.

Scratch took the bottle of bennies out his coat pocket and popped the top. He poured the last four into the palm of his hand, threw his head back, and swallowed. He coughed once, his eye became large again, and the black circles under both sockets dipped to his cheekbone. He touched the patch on his right eye and adjusted it.

"Who is that man?" Betty asked.

Scratch patted Betty's knee. "Nobody you need to worry about," he said.

The moonlight gave Betty a glimpse of Shaw's pock-marked face. Betty sighed. "I don't like the way he looks," she said.

Scratch chortled. "His mother didn't either," he opened the car door and stepped out. "That's why she gave him away. Stay in the car. No matter what happens."

He slammed the door and slowly walked toward Shaw, who was now leaning against his '42 Buick.

"Heyyy," he greeted Scratch. "You tried to sneak up on me. Niggers is hard to see in the dark." He chuckled. "If it weren't for the moonlight, y'know…"

"The insults are not funny," Scratch said.

"Not meant to be, boy," Shaw said.

"Why blackmail me?" Scratch asked.

"You have a lot to lose, son," Shaw said. "And you know how old man Spiff feels about you darkies. Hell, he's done everything he could to keep your people down."

"What about your boss? Every time he catches a criminal, the man's skin is darker than his," Scratch said. "I'm curious as how you knew about me and Immy."

Shaw breathed in and breathed out heavily. He said angrily: "You never mind how I know. I just know about you – and your family."

"I'm glad you have that knowledge about me," Scratch said. "I think it's only right I let you know I've sent your blackmail notes to Rooster."

"Bullshit," Shaw chuckled. "You ain't done that. You didn't know it was me…"

"You didn't bleach that typing paper good enough, Shaw," Scratch said. "Still had Coleman County plastered on the heading."

Shaw didn't know to say to that. His bottom lip trembled as his pea brain worked out what to say or do. After a bit, he finally blurted out: "You bring the damn money or what?"

"What!" Dobro said.

He came from behind with a stocking full of rocks. He swung, catching Shaw on the side of his temple. The rocks put a huge dent over his right eyebrow. Shaw staggered slightly then steadied himself upright and planted his feet. Shaw launched a barrage of rights to Dobro's midsection and a left hook knocked him flat on his ass. The stocking came out of Dobro's hand and the rocks tore through the nylon and hit the ground like birdshot.

Scratch turned his .38 upside-down, butt end up, and whacked Shaw on the right side of his head. Shaw squealed and turned quickly towards Scratch. He fell face-first in the dirt. Dobro stood and leaned against Shaw's car. He caught his breath, kept pointing without saying anything.

"You got what we need?" Scratch asked.

Dobro nodded quickly, trying to catch his breath, still pointing.

"We'll put them in Shaw's car. You drive," Scratch said. "Why do you keep pointing?" Finally Scratch turned to see and the headlights from his '48 Dodge put the lake, Shaw, Dobro, and Scratch in the spotlight. Scratch took off in a sprint, waving his hands, but it was too late.

"Your girlfriend stole your car," Dobro said.

24

Scratch lay in a ditch, his head bleeding profusely. The morning sun slashed his eyes like daggers through a ripe tomato.

"You fucked up, boy," Scratch heard a voice say. He cringed at the sound of the expletive. Blurriness gave way to a figure highlighted by the sun's rays. The old Korean man stood in front of Scratch, smiling, showing broken teeth and lips parted with blood spilling down his chin. "You fucked up, boy," the old Korean mouthed, but Scratch knew that wasn't his voice.

The old Korean man faded away like most ghosts do, but Scratch knew he'd be back, and like most ghosts, they never leave your side, always attached like umbilical cords that can never be severed.

Dozen stood over the ditch looking down at Scratch. He shook his head and repeated: "You fucked up, boy."

"Dozen," Scratch greeted him.

"You know how you got here?" Dozen said.

"No," Scratch rose slightly and surveyed his surroundings.

Behind Dozen was the black Cadillac parked sideways. All the doors were wide open, Homer's bodyguards stood at the front and rear of the car. Only Heilke sat in the backseat, her legs hanging out the car, spread wide for all to see she wasn't wearing any panties, and one of her stockings, that wasn't attached to her garter, had rolled down past her knee.

"All I know is you knuckleheads came into Homer's club, you saw somebody there and you two fuckin' chased him out."

"I don't remember. Who was he?"

"Some white kid. I didn't even know a kid was there let alone some cracker. He fuckin' shot up the place. Good thing Wolfy stopped him from shootin' any customers. But not before he caught a bullet."

"Is Wolfy OK?" Scratch asked.

"Yeah. He's OK. Just grazed his arm. Who the fuck was that white kid?"

"I don't know. I don't remember anything, except..." Scratch stopped himself. He started to tell what he and Dobro was doing at the lake. Driving Shaw into town, and Betty running off with his car. Then it came to him.

Betty was in with Shaw blackmailing him and Immy. But another question hit Scratch. Hit him hard. One that kept trying to pop into his brain and he kept trying to fight the question off. Was there something else Shaw and Betty were blackmailing Immy about? Could they have risked it all because Scratch was passing as white and he and Immy killed their father? Truth be told, Scratch had just realized that Uncle Homer might have helped cover up the killing. The passing as white, well, if he had thought about it, even old man Spiff would've covered that up just to save face in the white community because Scratch was in his employ.

Scratch was going to have to have to talk to Immy again.

"I don't remember a thing about last night, Dozen."

"Hmmm..." Dozen knew Scratch was holding back on him. "If you say so, motherfucker. All I know, it better not come back on me!"

"I'm hungry," Heilke said. "I want to eat at Dirty Joe's."

"You can eat anywhere you want, baby," Dozen leaned in and Heilke helped him climb on her. Her hands cradled the lower half of Dozen, and he struggled for a moment to stay there. They gave each other erotic, wet kisses that made everyone feel either disgusted or uncomfortable. Dozen slid down Heike's body, his hands cupping her breasts as his tiny feet were firmly planted on the ground. Dozen giggled childishly.

Something was different in Dozen's actions. His pose, the way he spoke, and the way the bodyguards responded to him.

"He's dead, isn't he?" Scratch said.

Dozen twirled around quickly. "Whatchu think, fool?"

Scratch didn't answer. He didn't get out of the ditch. Instead, he turned his head and laid his face in the dirt. Tears trickled down his chin, and his body convulsed. He didn't want Dozen or his men to see him cry, but there was no containing the emotions that took over.

Dozen sighed. His face showed empathy. Dozen slid down the muddy slope.

"Boss be careful!" one of the bodyguards yelled.

"Shut the hell up!" Dozen yelled back. "I got this! This is why I'm in charge, motherfucker!"

Scratch continued to weep, rolling his face in the dirt.

"Hey, stop that, man," Dozen told him. He sat on the side of the ditch. He massaged Scratch's back, rubbing in circular movements. "Get your face all dirty? C'mon. The boys are watchin'." Scratch became motionless except the heavings. Dozen continued: "I know... I know you're all tore up – who wouldn't be? Your uncle. Ya' know how I feel about Homer." Dozen clucked his tongue, and shook his head. "He was the only one who gave a damn about me. My own parents abandoned me. Left me with Charlie Diggers. Remember that asshole? He was the postman. He wouldn't stop beatin' me or his little girl Rae. Mother fucker who couldn't keep his hands off other people's women. Neighbor took care of him. Homer saw me getting' ready to stick up a gas station. If he hadn't stopped me, that cop who was hiding behind the building would've got me. Off and on, I worked with him ever since that. He never made fun of me. Never."

Scratch rose to a sitting position. He wiped dirt from his face. It smeared under his eyes, marking the dark circles even darker.

"He finally did himself in," Scratch said. "It was inevitable."

"Naw." Dozen made a face. 'He didn't kill himself. Some knotty-headed skinny punk shot him."

"Light-skinned boy?" Scratch asked.

"Yeah," Dozen said. "You know him?"

"If it's the same guy… yeah. I know he lives with his grandma. I can stake her place out…"

"Don't have to," Dozen released that childish giggle. "Get in the car. We got him."

"You got him?" Scratch asked.

"Yeah." Dozen snorted. "The dumbass came right in the window of Homer's study and shot him twice in the chest while he was reading *Moby Dick*. Damn, I just realized something."

Scratch watched Heilke slide to the left against the door. She pulled the flaps of her skirt up and flashed Scratch before she smoothed them out. He got in next to her.

"What's that?"

"Homer been readin' that damn book for 10 years."

25

Sure enough, Uncle Homer was dead.

He was sitting in his chair at his desk, slumped to the left, two bullet holes in his chest, a hardback copy of Moby Dick in his hand. Scratch fought the emotions that started take him over again. He fought back the tears. He'd stopped at the threshold of Homer's study, and Dozen urged him to go further. Scratch slowly sidled up to Homer's desk.

He took his fedora off in a half-hearted salute, closed his eyes and said a prayer in tribute, asking God to forgive Homer, watch over his soul. Scratch sighed, reopened his eyes and placed his fedora back on his balding head. A manila folder caught his eyes.

"What's this?" Scratch asked Dozen.

Dozen came around the desk, pushed an orange crate against the mahogany wood leg. He stepped on the crate for a better view.

"I don't know," Dozen said. "Looks like names and something about Cherry Tree Hill."

"The cemetery?" Scratch was shocked. "What business would he have to do with a cemetery?"

Dozen shrugged. "Hell if I know. Cherry Tree Hill. On Route One. That's what it says."

"Let me see," Scratch took the folder from Dozen. He read further down.

Two things popped up. Agatha Cripes died last year. She was killed in a hit-and-run. The Cripes family hired Scratch to find the driver.

Guy by the name of Morley Gates was driving drunk and sideswiped Agatha on the sidewalk.

"These names are people buried there," Scratch said.

"You gotta be kidding me!" Dozen exclaimed.

"Pinnacle is the company doing business with Homer."

"For what?" Then Dozen thought about it. "Oh, shit. The apartments he said he was building. Set to happen in a few months."

"Land," Scratch said. "They're going to move those bodies out their graves.

"You know what, he did mention he had a job for Pita-Paul and the boys. Just good old-fashioned hard work involved. I didn't know what he meant until now."

"I've been meaning to talk to you about Pita-Paul," Scratch said.

"He's been hanging around that jackass redneck governor. Yeah, I know. Homer sent him to work with that Klansman Gilmore."

Scratch glared at Dozen. "So this whole racist thing is a front?"

"Hell, naw," Dozen said. "That shit is real. Two things add to the mix. One: to keep us colored folk separated from the whites and make sure we never get up in the world."

"What's the second thing?" Scratch asked.

"Money. You know your damn self that money speaks louder than a kind word," Dozen said. "If a person can make money off of you, you think they give a shit about the color of your skin? Those apartments are low-rent, meant to be gutter houses. For Pinnacle, make bucketloads of money on rent, electric, and water. For Homer, it's a chance to make money off of whores and the shit people put in their bodies."

"How does Governor Adams fit in this?"

Dozen tilted his head sideways and cut his eyes at Scratch. "How do you think?" He threw his arms in the air. "Zoning laws. Moving the bodies out of the cemetery without it getting in the news."

"Whoa," Scratch said. A lightbulb just came on in his head. "I know why Horace Hammock was murdered."

Dozen gasped. "I thought he committed suicide!"

Scratch shook his head. "No," he said. He looked at his shoes but he was seeing a train of thought, or thoughts, running amok in his head. "Spiff asked me to look into it. He demanded I look into it. He was generally concerned about the situation."

"You sure your boy Spiff ain't behind that?"

"No, Dozen. Like I said, he was kind of angry about it. Concerned. Maybe," Scratch looked up at Dozen. "Scared."

"Oh, shit," Dozen said. "When a powerful motherfucker like Oliver Spiff gets scared, we all should be scared. Can't trust any damned soul. What the hell is the world coming to?"

"Boss," one of the bodyguards called out from the doorway.

"Yeah," Dozen called back in a shrill voice.

"We're ready," the bodyguard answered, then went back to the foyer.

"Ready for what?" Scratch asked.

Dozen raised an eyebrow. "Trial and execution."

He ushered Scratch out of Homer's office and into the foyer. They took some steps by the kitchen and pantry that led down a dark basement. The smell of black mold, cigarettes, and death entered Scratch's nostrils. Scratch retched a little and covered his mouth and nose. He heard Dozen giggling behind him.

"Yeah, Scratch, somebody had an accident down here," Dozen said. "Actually, quite a few people had several accidents."

Scratch guessed there were three other people in the basement. Not being able to see anything, brought on memories and anxieties. Part of Scratch knew where he was but another part of him feared a light would turn on and reveal he was be tied to a chair and that old Korean man was standing over him with hot shrapnel ready to slide it into the wound on Scratch's leg.

A familiar smell assaulted Scratch's nostrils. Hair relaxer and Barman's Vex, a popular aftershave with young black men in Darktown. He heard sobbing. Begging. A loud scream echoed. Scratch knew the voice.

"I didn't mean to kill no one," Felix Crump said. He sobbed more, tried to correct that with a manly, "So what?", but he was already broken and the sobbing interrupted his short attempt at being tough or hard. "It was just a game, I swear –I didn't know what I was doin'... Please... please..."

Scratch stood on the last step, Dozen snickering behind him. One naked light bulb connected to a tangled wire swung back and forth making everyone's shadows bigger than their souls. One of Dozen's henchmen had a long jagged-bladed knife, the kind used for gutting fish. The blade sliced Felix's chest, dragged across other knife wounds. He screamed as his skin opened up and revealed what was inside him. Felix gurgled and whined. His body convulsed from going into shock.

Scratch turned his head. Then he pushed Dozen out of the way and trotted up the stairs.

"Scratch!" Dozen called out. "Scratch! C'mon! I thought you'd like to see some justice for your uncle's murder!"

"There are steps for doing that, Dozen. Laws."

Dozen snorted contemptuously. "White man's laws. You know how we do things in Darktown. We don't need laws invented by white people. We take care of our own, no matter how... unpleasant the shit is."

"You said you know where my car is."

"Scratch, you can stay here... work for me. I ain't Homer. You can trust me."

Scratch was silent. He didn't even look at Dozen.

"OK," Dozen said softly, patting Scratch on his lower back. "I'll get Zeke to drive you. Not far from your sister's house."

"Drivable?" Scratch asked.

"Yeah. You can drive it. From what I understand, your girlfriend is in Mercy Hospital."

"Why did they take her there and not Johnson Medical?"

"She didn't want to be in a hospital with negroes," Dozen said. "Her words."

26

It seemed Scratch couldn't get away from that Frank Sinatra song *In the Wee Small Hours of the Morning*. The radio in the Cadillac was blaring it and Zeke was furiously trying to match the volume.

Zeke kept trying to start up a conversation, but Scratch wasn't interested. He would either nod, grunt, or answer in one-word sentences. For the first time in a long time, Scratch didn't care what happened next. He didn't care if he ever solved the case, he didn't care what was in the hatbox. He didn't give a rat's ass about Oliver Spiff.

He did want to see Betty. For some reason, he wanted to see her, let her know he wasn't mad about her taking his car, or helping Shaw blackmail him and Immy. He wanted to tell her he loved her. None of this shit mattered.

No one mattered.

Not Spiff. Not Shaw. Not Homer. Or any-fucking-body in Odarko, or Darktown. Just them. Betty and Allan. I'd let her call me Allan, if she wanted…

"Hey look, Allan," Zeke said, looking at Scratch in the rearview mirror. "I know we have some bad blood, but I ain't holding no grudges against you."

Scratch snorted. "That's good to know."

"C'mon, motherfucker." Zeke was exasperated. "I'm tryin' to be amicable. Pleasant, even. Make up, and all that shit, and all I get from you is high-hat."

"Sorry I'm hurting your feelings," Scratch said.

Zeke sighed, shook his head. "Lord, Jesus. There ain't no getting' through to this son of a bitch. All he wants to do is agitate me. What should I do?"

Is he talking to me or who? Scratch thought.

"What the hell are you doing?" he asked.

Scratch had to ask. He'd never witnessed anyone doing that except old Miss Winters, the woman who used to help look after him and Immy sometimes when his mother worked late. She had her hands lifted, eyes raised to the sky, asking God, or Jesus what was wrong with her life. Sometimes the conversation was 20 minutes, sometimes it was four hours. Old Miss Winters never let anyone interrupt her talks with a higher being to sort things out.

"You mind? I'm talkin' to Jesus, not you!" Zeke raised his voice. "So sit back, and shut up!"

"I don't mind you talking to Jesus," Scratch said. "Just don't talk to him about me, especially in front of me."

"You ain't got no choice, Jack," Zeke said. Scratch saw large brown eyes with burning embers staring at him in the rear-view mirror. "Now, we can stop this car right now, and I help you get closer to Jesus and you can ask him how he feels about this conversation. But you'll also be tasting rare earth from a grave. Your choice, Jack."

Scratch didn't have anything to say to that. Mere seconds later, a bizarre spectacle would catch his eye.

The Cadillac eased into the town square. A body was hanging from a flagpole in front of the post office and the general store. The body swung back and forth in the gentle morning breeze. A noose of thick, coarse rope was around the man's broken neck, and his flopping arms were tied loosely behind his back. At first, Scratch thought the Klan had slipped in late at night and strung up somebody from Darktown, as they had done a few years ago, and when he was a little boy. Seeing a lynching always made Scratch feel sick to his stomach.

But the closer the Cadillac got to the scene, the easier it was to see the body hanging from the flag pole was a white man. Then Scratch saw his uniform. Instantly he realized it was Deputy Shaw. Overwhelming guilt slid up from the pit of Scratch's stomach and rose up into a lump in his throat. Only... it had been him or Shaw. Or had it? Could it have gone another way?

Probably not.

Events from last night came to Scratch in snapshots.

Then they'd fade away and a migraine would start. All Scratch could see in his mind was the old Korean man screaming at him and spitting in his face. The Korean man smacked Scratch. He showed Scratch a long, thin stick and pointed it at Scratch's eye. The stick touched the surface of Scratch's eyeball and he jerked away. The Korean man smacked Scratch on his left shoulder with the stick. Scratch screamed.

The Cadillac stopped.

Zeke turned completely around in his seat and glared at Scratch.

"What the hell is wrong with you?" Zeke demanded.

"What?"

"You back there hollering like somebody chopped off your big toe or something!"

Scratch rubbed his face, removed his fedora, rubbed his head and returned the fedora, lowering the brim over his eyes.

"Nothing, Zeke," Scratch said. "Don't worry about it."

"Oh, I'm gonna worry about it," Zeke shook his head pityingly. "Got a crazy person in the backseat..."

"We're a pretty pair," Scratch chuckled. "You talkin' to Jesus and me screaming at ghosts."

Zeke snorted. "Yeah, only Jesus is real. Ghosts ain't."

Scratch thought about that. Profound or a foolish thing to say? He didn't know the answer any more than Zeke did, except Zeke was sure of what he was saying and nothing could shake him loose of his faith. Scratch was a whole other animal altogether. His faith or faiths, or lack of, could always be challenged, and dismantled with a whisper or an atomic explosion.

"Why'd you stop the car?" Scratch asked.

"We at your car, fool," Zeke said. "Look yonder."

Betty hadn't gotten far. The lake was on the right, but the road she took would have led her back into Darktown. The '48 Dodge was parked in front of the church. The front end was bent to hell. Other than that, the car was in remarkable shape to have been in a head-on collision.

"Thanks for the ride," Scratch opened the door.

"Hold up," Zeke said. "Look under the backseat."

Scratch reached under and put a hand on hard cardboard. He pulled out a hatbox.

"Dozen was going to give it to you," Zeke said. "But you ran out before he could."

"Where he get it?"

"Me and Moses found it next to your car," Zeke replied.

"My car is in good shape to have hit another car," Scratch said.

"Who told you that?"

"Dozen."

"He don't know. He wasn't there," Zeke said. "Me and Moses was sitting in this Cadillac drinking some rum. We went to collect from a few businessmen. We were sittin' right here. Your car came up. I said, 'Hey, Moses. Look, it's old Scratch burnin' up the roads.' Moses said, 'He got to be runnin' from a woman's old man or from a woman!' We laughed hard at that. I'm sure the rum had its effect on our sense of humor. Your car sailed by us and swiped a tree. Your girl got out and started running. This red Fury came hot-trottin' and WHAM! Caught your girl, sent her sky-high.

"That's when this '53 Crestline came up and chased that Fury."

That was Shaw's car, Scratch thought. Dobro and me must've been in it, taking Shaw to his fate.

"I could've swore I saw you in that car. I just shook my head and wondered why the hell you weren't driving that '48 Dodge you love so much? Then again, ain't none of it my business."

Scratch didn't say anything. He wanted to say thank you and you've been a big help. Scratch didn't like Zeke at all. Never did. He tried to date Immy when they were all younger. All he was interested in was having sex with Immy. He was abusive in the way he talked to her and Scratch always suspected the bruises on Immy's arms were because of Zeke.

"I know who owns that Crestline," Zeke said.

"Oh yeah?" Scratch said. "Who?"

"Deputy Sheriff from Coleman County." Zeke sneered. "Naw, I told myself. Scratch Williams don't deal with those boys from Coleman County. Just Odarko. That's why I thought it was strange I thought I saw you in that car. Hmph! It was dark and I was drunk as hell. I was just seeing things."

"How do you know it was Shaw's car?"

"Your uncle had some dealings with him before," Zeke said, picking at a nostril with a long thumbnail. When it hit on something, he flinched and withdrew the thumbnail. "And... I've seen him go in Immy's house a bunch of times. Looks like she likes guys with your pale complexion." Zeke laughed. "Shit, I saw him picking up Immy yesterday."

Scratch felt anger pulsating through his veins. Zeke could see it in his eyes. Zeke was a little afraid. He wasn't the confident Jesus-talking street punk he appeared to be a few minutes before.

"Hey, Scratch." Zeke fumbled his words nervously. "I have to get. Dozen has some things for me to do... Uh... do me a favor?"

"What?" Scratch growled.

"Don't open that hatbox until I'm way down the road."

"I haven't even thought about opening it..." Scratch looked down at the hatbox sitting between his legs. He considered tossing it in the ditch and telling Spiff any lie that popped into his head. Nothing mattered anyway. When he got through with Immy, they were going to hang him for her murder. "Yeah, Zeke," Scratch said, opening the car door. "I'll wait until I see your exhaust pipe before I open this box."

Zeke smiled and waved to Scratch. Scratch slammed the door, and the Cadillac roared off.

Scratch stood in the street, holding one of two hatboxes that had caused death, humiliation, and a whole lot of misery.

27

He stared at the box for a long time.

It sat on the dashboard of his '48 Dodge. An ominous, eerie feeling came over Scratch. Thoughts of the events of the past week entered his mind. Some things just didn't add up. People involved in this case – cases, actually – and their motives didn't make sense. Old man Spiff sends Scratch to make sure his daughter's boyfriend gets out of town. The boyfriend is murdered after a fight with Scratch and no one is in a hurry to solve the murder. Someone hits Scratch from behind and takes his glass eye. Teenagers are riding around in a red Fury killing pillars of Odarko and Darktown..? Why? The owner of a newspaper commits suicide and old man Spiff wants that investigated as a murder. Why? He himself is blackmailed by Shaw, and thinks Betty is in on it, but turns out...

Scratch sighed. Closed his eyes. "Really Immy was his partner," Scratch opened his eyes and smacked the steering wheel. "Why, Immy? Why?"

And how does this hatbox fit in with it all?

"Wait," Scratch said aloud. "That's not the same hatbox."

Same black vinyl box, minus the gold initials SS. Zeke had warned him not to open the box around him. Why?

"I know," Scratch said to himself. "I'm asking a lot of questions, and so far I have come up with few answers."

He sat the hatbox on the seat next to him and took the lid off. At first, Scratch was dumbfounded. When he realized what was in the hatbox, tears formed in his eyes. Bones. Skeletal remains of a baby wrapped in a discolored cloth. He quickly placed the lid back on the hat bot and shoved it across the seat far away from him.

Scratch broke down again, weeping hard, shaking his head violently.

28

Immy opened the front door of her house and discovered Pita-Paul standing in her kitchen. He stepped aside and she saw Gilmore sitting at her kitchen table, his leg in its plaster cast propped on another chair. She dropped her bag of groceries on the floor. A loaf of bread fell out, followed by two apples and a chicken breast.

"You didn't think you'd see us, huh?" Gilmore said.

Immy turned to run out the front door, but two Oklahoma Highway Patrolmen appeared on the threshold. She back-pedaled, stepped out of her left heel and tripped. Immediately she burst into tears.

"I don't know anything," Immy said, sniffles slurring her words. "I don't know anything."

"Come on, you don't expect us to believe that? You and that deputy from Coleman County was blackmailing everybody!" Gilmore laughed, his eyes surveying the disarray of the house. "By the looks of it, he got most of the damn money. Your dark meat must not have been that special."

"I don't know anything," she repeated.

Gilmore snarled and snapped his fingers. Pita-Paul shuffled over and kicked Immy in the ribs. She screamed and rolled over on her back, holding her left side. Immy had several coughing fits. Pita-Paul was about to kick her again when Gilmore snapped his fingers again. Pita-Paul put his foot back on the floor and went back to a rigid stance.

"Give me one of those apples," Gilmore barked an order at one of the OHPs. The highway patrolman hopped to it, scooped up the bruised red apple and marched it over to Gilmore. Gilmore looked the apple over and took a huge bite of it. "You been in the town square yet?" Gilmore asked, chewing vigorously.

Immy shook her head, weeping silently.

Gilmore swallowed, didn't waste time taking another bite of the apple. He chewed quickly, sloppily. Bits of apple fell to the front of his shirt. He swallowed hard and glared at Immy. "Shaw is swinging from a pole for all the niggers in Darktown to see."

That disturbed Immy's weeping for a moment. She managed to say: "What-what do you mean?"

"Your boyfriend! The one who's married to a skinny, tiny little woman and has three small kids – they live at a house on Berget Street in Coleman County! The white man you been fuckin' since the middle of last year! He's dead..." He pointed the apple at Immy. "You two were stupid as shit. Can you believe this?" He asked Pita-Paul. The question fell on deaf ears. So he directed his enquiry to the state patrolmen. "Can you believe this shit? They try to blackmail the governor of Oklahoma. Not just him, but all these people involved in dirty pictures. Holy shit... it's... beguiling. I know – big word for me – but I'm always intrigued – there I go again, oops, flauntin' my college education from the U of Oklahoma – again, let me say, in a way that a nigger can understand. People who think they can get somethin' from those who control everything, and think that their brains are so big and get these ideas, the devil planted those ideas in their heads. The devil is a nigger, you know that, right? God is on our side, the white man. What I'm tryin' to say, is you got two strikes against you to make sure you won't get ahead in life. 1: You're a nigger. Plain and simple. 2: You're a woman..." He let the words trail off. Gilmore sighed deeply. He shook his head and laughed. "I mean, don't you understand that you are a nigger, which means dumb to begin with, right? Yes, yes, yes, yes... it does. I mean, I see what Shaw liked in you. I mean, if I liked nigger women, that is," The state patrolmen laughed along with Gilmore.

"You're almost white. But you aren't. I have to know something. What fascinates me is when two dumb people get together to hatch a plan to move them up in society. You see, Shaw, he was as dumb as they came. I know, I played against him in high school football. He was a quarter-back and I was on defense, and all we had to do was make out like we were going the left and he would throw to the right, and there I was, with an interception. Every time. One game, I had four touchdowns." Everyone laughed but Pita-Paul. He stared blankly at Gilmore. "How did you and Shaw know about the governor being involved with that kidnapping of that old actress's baby?"

Immy got herself together. She fixed her dress, moved strands of light brown hair from her face. She raised up, but stayed on her knees. "His sister told us about it."

"Who's his sister?" Gilmore asked. He looked at Immy as if she were lying. "I didn't know Shaw had any siblings. I just remember he was an only child."

"Betty Klein," Immy said.

Gilmore laughed. "She's a Jew. Shaw ain't Jewish. You're making this up."

She stood, kicked off her right high heel. She smiled at Gilmore al-luringly. She batted her eyes and licked her lips seductively. Gilmore wasn't interested. He scowled. From the look on his face, he was dis-gusted by Immy. "No, he told me he was. Shaw was adopted when he was five. Betty was two. His father was a gambler from New Jersey. They moved here to get away from the mob. His father owed a lot of money. Somebody came down here and shot his father and mother. Left him and Betty in the house with their dead parents. When they got adopted, she was shipped off to an orphanage in Texas. He stayed here."

"I'm supposed to believe that bullshit?" Gilmore said. The two OHPs laughed and he joined in for the last chorus.

"It's not bullshit!" Immy protested.

"Really," Gilmore shook his head and waved his hands at Immy. "Really don't matter. We're off the subject. So, you two were blackmailing fucking everyone. I mean, huge balls! Blackmailing Homer? Blackmailing the pervert druggist? Even damn Oliver Spiff. That's unbelievable. It's a wonder him or Homer didn't have you two killed..." Gilmore stopped talking. A smirk crossed his chipmunk face. "Wait a minute. They didn't know who was blackmailing them. Well, I'll be a monkey's... No, your breed are monkeys. I'll be damned. What the hell did you do with the money you two got?"

"Real estate." Immy swallowed hard. "We invested in real estate."

"Talking about around here, in nigger town?"

Immy nodded slowly.

"Uh-huh," Gilmore said. He thought about what she said. "You invested in that rival company?"

Immy slowly nodded again. Her hands started to shake.

"You invested with Reliance," Gilmore said. "The bid hasn't even closed..."

"It has," Immy cut him off.

"Oh," Gilmore said, sorrowfully.

"No one has made it public yet," Immy said.

"You invested in a company who plans to build up Darktown," Gilmore stood, pointing the half-eaten apple at her. "Give your kind a university, supermarkets, dry cleaners, a shopping center, etcetera, etcetera, etcetera. Make the world better for niggers. Truth be told, it's all about money. Everything is. Always has been, always will be."

Immy tried to weigh options and realized she had none. Pita-Paul had the bedroom covered, the patrolmen had the front door blocked, and Gilmore stood in the way to get through the kitchen and out the back door.

"The governor's company Green Hills plans to do the same thing. You knew that." he approached Immy one small step at a time, dragging that leg in its cast. "Why didn't you put that money with a winner? I mean, he cares for your kind, too. More so than that rinky-dink Reliance Oil company. They ain't for people's rights. I should know. I had dealings with them and Spiff, who by the way is in cahoots with..." Gilmore burst out laughing. "Holy shit. You used the money

Spiff paid you off to invest in a company that's tied to him. *You have big balls*, negress!" He shrugged. "I have a question for you."

"OK – OK," Immy said.

"What were you blackmailing Spiff for? I'm surprised his yardbird didn't come after you."

"His yardbird wouldn't hurt me," Immy said. "I don't tell people's secrets."

"Is that so? You have a special relationship with him, too, huh? You like your men white, I see. Come on, you can tell me now. Really won't make a difference," Gilmore chuckled.

"Shaw heard Spiff and his daughter," Immy said slowly. "They were in a… relationship unbecoming of society."

"Is that so?" Gilmore laughed. "You know, you two dummies might have hit on something. Thing is, I started hearing a rumor about that when I worked with the union. Hmph! Must have been some truth to it!"

Gilmore nodded and the two patrolmen grabbed Immy by her arms. She cried out and kicked at anyone close by. Gilmore wagged a finger at Pita-Paul. Gilmore shoved the half-eaten apple in her mouth. Immy moaned, sobbed hard. Pita-Paul took out a switchblade from his pants pocket, showed Immy the blade. She squirmed, gurgled, let out a muffled scream.

"Hey, boys, y'all like brown meat? I hear it tastes good," Gilmore laughed.

A bedroom door creaked open. The sound caught the attention of the Patrolman on the left. He turned and saw the barrel of a Smith and Wesson .38 poke through the crack of the door. Just as he was about to say something, the gun went off. A bullet caught the patrolman in the right side of his temple. Blood splattered Immy and Pita-Paul, blinding him temporarily.

Immy tore loose from the other patrolman and kicked Pita-Paul square in his crotch. He fell to his knees screaming like a wounded animal. She spat the apple out and screamed like a banshee as she tried to run away. Gilmore reached out for her, took hold of the front of Immy's dress and tore the fabric, exposing cocoa-colored skin against a white lacy brassiere. He bent down at the same time to pick up the switchblade. Immy pulled away from Gilmore's grip and her dress ripped all the way to the waist.

Scratch stepped out the bedroom, aimed the .38 and fired twice at the patrolman. Two bullets ripped through the patrolman's chest just as he unholstered his .357 Magnum. The patrolman fell on his back with a loud grunt.

Immy saw Gilmore maneuver slowly toward a hutch to use as leverage to stand. She sprinted over and pushed the hutch on top of Gilmore's legs. He cried out in agony as knick-knacks and dishes fell around him. Immy used the distraction to head to the kitchen. Gilmore reached out and grabbed Immy's ankle, his torn, jagged, filthy fingernails tearing into the nylon stocking on Immy's right leg. Immy fell, turned herself around and started to kick Gilmore in the neck and face with her other foot. Gilmore took the punishment. He pulled Immy closer to him.

By this time, Pita-Paul had gotten himself together. He rushed Scratch, tackling him with all his strength. Scratch thought he'd been hit by a freight train. The.38 flew out of Scratch's hands and landed near the dead patrolmen. Scratch covered his face to block punches from Pita-Paul and felt nasty stings to his wrists. He didn't stop there. Pita-Paul gave Scratch several rabbit punches to his midsection, each blow feeling like bricks slamming against his kidneys.

Finally, Immy got away from Gilmore. She grabbed a stucco pot that had been sitting on the hutch. She brought it down hard on Gilmore's head. He cried out as his skull cracked open. But that wasn't enough for her. Immy came down hard on Gilmore's skull again, and again, until he was no longer moving, just breathing shallowly.

He was a bloody mess.

Scratch had no chance to get to the gun. He did see the switchblade was close to him. He took one more driving fist to the chest. With all his strength, Scratch grabbed the switchblade and drove the blade into Pita-Paul's left eye. Pita-Paul screamed. He crouched, arms flailing but kept his balance. He back-pedaled and fell on his back, moaning and wailing.

Scratch and Immy trotted to Pita-Paul. They stood over him and listened to a man as big as a redwood tree weep like a baby. Words tumbled out of Pita-Paul's fluttering mouth. A mixture of German and English. It was then that Scratch realized that Pita-Paul was just a huge retarded child locked in a man's body. All these years people thought he didn't know English. He understood English and he could speak it – just not as plainly as everyone else.

"I'm sorry, Allan," Immy closed her eyes and leaned against the wall.

"Why, Immy? Why did you do all this – and blackmail me..?"

"No, that part was made up."

"I got the letters, Immy."

"Yeah, but Shaw used me. For some reason he and Betty held out on me. They never invested in any land deal. They kept all the money for themselves. I needed to get even with him. So I wrote the letters on paper from the Colman police department."

Scratch sighed. "You knew I would take care of him."

"Yes, Allan," Immy nodded. "I knew you'd take care of him."

"Where are the kids?" Scratch said without looking at her.

"A friend has them," Immy said.

"Get changed," Scratch told her. "Grab what you want to take with you. I'm driving you to Oklahoma City."

"I don't..."

"No time to argue, Immy! They were going to kill you! The governor will surely try again!"

Immy nodded as she started to weep. "I know," she said. "I know."

29

Scratch got Immy and her kids to Oklahoma City safely. He got a room at the Charlton, paid for a month. No words were spoken, no hugs, no kisses, no goodbyes. He stopped at the General Hospital to see Betty. It was a terrible sight.

He sat in a metal folding chair a nurse provided. He stared at Betty, taking in her condition, for a long time. No words were spoken. He wanted to tell her he loved her. He wanted to tell her he forgave her. But his tongue wouldn't release the words.

Betty was in a coma. Bandaged. Her arms and legs in casts. Scratch bawled like a baby. He couldn't help it. Too many things were happening at once, so much to feel, and he didn't want to feel anything.

"You killed Horace Hammock," Scratch wiped his nose and eye. "You killed him, came back, and that's when I surprised you. What were you looking for?" He waited for an answer. No answer came, of course, and Scratch continued in one feverish sentence. "His evidence that you, Shaw and Immy were blackmailing everyone. That part I was sure of... he also had the hatbox with-with the bones of the baby..."

Scratch wept hard.

"Why didn't you come to me?" he said, sobbing. "You could've told me... I could have taken care of everything..."

The nurse came into the room, stood in the threshold and listened to Scratch weep. She backed out of the room and closed the door.

* * *

On his way back to Odarko, three Oklahoma Highway Patrolmen pulled him over. Guns were drawn, and one of the butts of their .357s found its way to Scratch's forehead.

When he came to, his eyes focused on two men sitting at a huge desk. One of the men was the governor of Oklahoma, the other was old man Spiff's lawyer. Guarding the door and the windows behind Adams were Oklahoma highway patrolmen, six to be exact, and all them with their weapons aimed at Scratch.

"You were out for quite a while," Dan Lowery said.

"He had to rest up," Governor Adams said. "He knew we got a lot of talkin' to do."

"What do we have to talk about, Governor?" Scratch asked. "Loyalty?" That question was lobbed at Lowery.

Lowery smiled at that. "Loyalty goes on as long as whoever is signing my paycheck."

"How long has that been going on?" Scratch picked himself up and used a chair to steady himself. He realized he'd left a dirty stain where he'd been lying on a red and yellow checkered rug with tassels at each corner.

"Inconsequential, Mister Williams," Lowery said.

"Lowery is a good man. An asset to anyone's business," Adams said, chuckled, his crooked teeth poking out between fat heart-shaped lips. His three chins moved up and down a gurgling, wobbling throat. Adams was a fat man. He was too big for the Columbus wingback chair he was propped up in. He looked as if he was desperately trying to recoup his youth by combing the three stands of hair over a huge bald spot and wearing a modern pair of men's thin eyeglass frames that barely covered his large fish eyes.

"That's what old man Spiff thinks of the young lawyer. Funny, though, Governor." Scratch sat in the glossy wooden chair in front of the desk. "If I may ask a question?"

Adams waved up a hand indifferently. "Ask away, Mister Williams."

"Knowing your views on human beings," Scratch lit a cigarette, blew smoke in the governor's direction. "What are you doing hanging around with a Jew?"

"Are there any better people to be around especially when it comes to law and business, Mister Williams? I know he's from unclean blood. I know. But I'm all right with it as long as he takes care of problems and brings me those greenbacks." He cleared his throat, readjusted his large ass in the chair. "I'll overlook anyone's deficiencies as long as I am compensated. Just as I'll overlook your deficiency."

"What deficiency is that?" Scratch asked.

Lowery and Adams looked each other and laughed.

"A nigger is always going to be a nigger no matter what skin color he pretends to be," Adams said, his thick dark eyebrows narrowed. "You can never run away from the truth."

"I have something of yours." Lowery rose from his chair next to Adams, took two steps and retrieved a glass eye from his jacket pocket. He tossed it to Scratch. Scratch caught it haphazardly with both hands. "I'm sure you've been missing this."

Scratch removed his eyepatch. He turned from Lowery and Adams, held his head to one side and eased his glass eye into the empty eye socket. He turned back to face Lowery and Adams. A highway patrolman stood in front of Scratch, the barrel of his .357 touching the tip of his nose. Scratch flinched, then gave an odd, twisted smile.

"Mighty big gun for little old me."

"Wanted to make sure you were not going to pull anything," Lowery said. "Now that you have your eye back. I noticed... there was a lack of confidence."

"All right, Patrolman," Adams spoke up. "Put the gun away. It's obvious Mr Williams is not going to try anything."

The patrolman holstered his gun and stepped quickly, even stiffly, back to his post by the window.

"OK, this is where I tell you what I know," Scratch said with a chuckle.

Lowery and Adams glanced at each other and laughed.

"We don't care about what you know, Mr Williams," Lowery said.

"I like this guy. He really thinks he can negotiate for his life," Adams added.

"If you wanted me dead," Scratch said. "You would already have killed me."

Adams sighed. "We'll humor you."

"You killed Gardner," Scratch said.

Lowery shrugged. "Inconsequential."

"You keep saying that, counselor. I bet you won't say it in front of a judge when you go on trial."

Adams laughed. "None of this so-called evidence will go to trial, Mr Williams."

"Even if you kill me," Scratch said to Adams. "Others know. Might take years. Eventually, you'll stand trial. You also burned down Betty Klein's house. I saw you out and about with the crowd. Some old lady stopped you. You burned down the house because of the film. You and the governor were having a great time with Felix, weren't you?"

Neither man said anything. They exchanged glances. Lowery swallowed hard and looked down at his 100-dollar shoes.

"I understand now. Blackmail all over the place. Somebody hired Gardner to film you two. Somebody hired Felix to show up at the Primrose. I saw the hole in the wall when I touched that hatbox. Gardner tried to stop me. He was killed, I was hit on the head. I woke up next to Gardner's body in my car out in Coleman County. Jerzy said highway patrolmen were all over the Primrose for hours. He was told not to go in either room. This thing ballooned, got out of whack for both of you." Scratch sniffed the air as he took a long drag from his cigarette and exhaled as if he was drawing his last breath. "I'm sure the governor would hate for his youthful step in the wrong direction to go public."

"What direction are you referring to, Mister Williams?" Adams asked with a smile. He was amused by the way the conversation had taken a turn or by the way Scratch had taken charge of the meeting.

"You and Homer, with Pita-Paul, kidnapped an aging movie star's baby. During the snatch, one of you shot and killed her husband. I'm not sure which one," Scratch cleared his throat. "My guess is… it was you, Governor."

"Oh." Adams's grin widened. "How so?"

"You really don't give a shit about people," Scratch said. "Homer cared just enough. Depending on what he could get out of it. You don't care how you get things. You just take, helping yourself to a man's last meal as you step over his body. You remind me of someone."

"You are a very resourceful man, Scratch Williams," Governor Adams said. "I think I should retain you."

"What?" Lowery was not only shocked by the governor's comment, but alarmed. "Are you sure about this, Governor? I think your first decision…"

"Shut up, you fork-tongued cretin!" Adams screamed. "I call the goddamn shots. You hear?"

Lowery didn't say a word. He wanted to. He was fuming, his nostrils flaring as he breathed rapidly.

"What makes you think you can take me away from Spiff?"

"Mister Williams, I'm already taking everything away from him. Surely having you as my personal yardbird would just amuse me."

The door flew open, knocking one patrolman to the floor. The other turned, drew his weapon. The barrel of a Smith and Wesson .45 appeared and fired once. The bullet sliced through the patrolman's gut like a knife through hot butter. He cried out, fell to his knees. Shep Howard peered through the cracked door. The patrolman who had fallen pulled his gun and fired at Shep. The bullet zipped by Shep's nose and took a huge chunk of the door frame with it.

Shep kicked the door open and stood a moment on the threshold and fired twice at the patrolman, both bullets lodged in his forehead, creating a chasm so big, a Coke bottle could fit inside the wound. Just for that fleeting second, everyone saw a gunfighter, not an aging lawman with bad knees. Bullets flew around the governor's office like mayflies around a pile of horse shit. Shep spun around and hid behind the door just as the bullets created a paint-by-numbers line drawing of a man in the moon. Scratch leaped from his chair. He fell to the floor and mashed his face to the carpet.

Mere minutes later, the gunplay ended. Five more patrolmen lay dead on the floor, drowning in their own blood. The other three more than likely killed by friendly fire than by Shep. Nothing happened for a few minutes. The only sounds in the room was sobbing coming from Lowery.

"Adams?" A voice called out. "You alive?"

Scratch recognized the voice. It was Oliver Spiff.

Governor Adams didn't answer.

The door riddled with bullet holes swung open. Shep stepped inside the office, gun aimed at anything that moved. George Spiff followed. When the coast was clear, Spiff stepped in front and surveyed the situation.

Shep helped Scratch to his feet. He looked behind the desk and saw Governor Adams dead. It seems a bullet had struck the governor in the chest.

"He's dead," Shep said.

"Hmm," Spiff thought about it. "That was not my intention."

"How do we handle this?" Shep asked.

"Call Terry at the American News Agency," Spiff said. "Say the governor has died of a heart attack."

"Yes sir," Shep said. He picked up the telephone and dialed. Spoke a few words, then hung up.

Lowery could still be heard blubbering, praying to a God he never worshipped. He was under the governor's desk curled up in a ball.

"Yardbird," Spiff said to Scratch. "Get that shit-kicker out from under the desk."

Scratch took a few steps to the side of the desk. He reached down and grabbed Lowery by the collar and dragged him out. Lowery screamed, whined, begged for them not kill him. Scratch jerked him hard, as if he had a disobedient dog on a leash. Lowery choked on his words, coughed, and vomited on the carpet.

Spiff looked away. No one was sure if he was disgusted by Lowery vomiting or his cowardice.

When Lowery was done retching, he looked up at Spiff and wept hard, his body convulsing as he tried to apologize.

"I'm so sorry, Mr Spiff. I'm so sorry. Please, please. Please, please, please, please...PLEASE DON'T KILL ME!"

Spiff laughed. It was a mean, hard laugh. Soul-crushing.

Lowery lowered his head into his hands and cried harder.

"I see what you tried to do," Spiff said. "If that was me lying on the floor," he pointed at Governor Adams. "You would be in charge of Pinnacle. Or at least you thought you would. No. I'm not going to kill you. Instead, I'm going to run you out of my town, my state. Run you out like the whipped cur you are. Shep, take this motherless dog and put him on a bus."

"As he is?" Shep asked.

"As he fucking is. He leaves the state of Oklahoma with the clothes on his back. Nothing else. Yardbird?"

"Yes, Mr Spiff?"

"Take his wallet. I don't want him to have any money I gave him."

30

The Chrysler Crown Imperial rolled down the highway toward Spiff's mansion. Scratch was in the backseat with Spiff and the old Korean man was sitting in the seat in front of them. The driver had the window rolled up, as per Spiff's orders. Just in case anything incriminating was said, Scratch figured. The radio was on. *Peggy Sue* by Buddy Holly ended and a newsman came on.

"We bring you this news with much sadness," the broadcaster said. He paused and you could hear in his voice how upset he was. "Governor Quincy Adams has passed away. He suffered a massive heart attack in his office and was brought to Oklahoma General, where he died shortly thereafter. This station will break for a moment of silence."

Scratch glanced at Spiff. He was grinning from ear to ear, smoking a cigar and drinking brandy. That was Spiff's expression of victory. Right on cue, the next song came on the radio. Hank Williams singing *You Win Again*. Scratch turned his attention to the old Korean man. He was singing along with the song.

> *The news is out, all over town*
> *That you've been seen, a-runnin' 'round.*
> *I know that I should leave, but then*
> *I just can't go, you win again.*

This heart of mine, could never see
What everybody knew but me.
Just trusting you was my great sin.
What can I do, you win again.

The old Korean man smiled, then disappeared.

Scratch looked out the window. He flinched. Something in the distance caught his eye. A car was turned upside down, half in a ditch, half lying on the blacktop with glass surrounding it. Scratch knocked on the glass of the driver's compartment. The driver lowered the window.

"Yes sir?" The driver asked.

"Stop the car!" Scratch ordered.

"What?" Spiff protested, slurring his words. "Burt! Don't you dare!?"

"Stop the car, Burt! There's an accident!" Scratch talked over Spiff.

"Sir?" Burt slowed the car down, but was confused about the orders.

Spiff let out a sigh of anxiety. "Will this amuse you, Scratch Williams?"

"Tickled pink, Oliver Spiff!"

"Then stop the damn car, Burt!" Spiff ordered.

Burt did as he was told.

Scratch got out of the limousine, not even waiting for the car to come to a full halt. Burt got out afterwards. They immediately investigated the accident. Spiff eventually got out, complaining non-stop. Scratch walked over slowly to look at the car. Burt went to the other side.

Scratch remembered the night before when he and Dobro chased this white kid through Dobro's club. Not just the kid they were after, the girl who was him...

A red Plymouth Fury was turned over, lying on its roof, all the glass from the windows, windshield and rear screen obliterated. The driver, a blond-haired male, hung out of the window, his face cut into ribbons and with one large glass shard piercing his throat. The second victim was a young brown-haired woman. She was sprawled out on the blacktop about 20 feet from the destroyed Fury. Her broken and mangled body was lying face down. Scratch went to look at the young woman, Burt close behind him. They both squatted down, Scratch doing so with a grunt. He turned the young woman's head to face him...

Scratch and Dobro had both been chasing Maggie Spiff, too. They couldn't catch her or the blond-haired boy because they ran into Pita-Paul and Gilmore right outside the club. Dobro managed to get away. The first blow from Pita-Paul made Scratch black out.

"This is preposterous," Oliver Spiff said, hurling his cigar down and mashing it into the blacktop with his shoe. "I need to get home and conduct business! Who cares who these people are..."

"Oh, my God," Burt choked back tears. "It's..."

"Maggie Spiff," Scratch finished Burt's sentence.

George Spiff rushed over to make sure they weren't pulling some kind of sick practical joke on him. No. It was Maggie Spiff who was lying dead in the middle of the road. Spiff cradled his daughter in his arms and begged Scratch and Burt to do something. Burt sprinted to the limousine and drove off to find the nearest phone.

"That's sad," the old Korean man said.

"Yeah," Scratch said.

"Did he win again?" the old Korean man asked. "And if he did, at what cost?"

Dear reader,

We hope you enjoyed reading *Yardbird*. Please take a moment to leave a review, even if it's a short one. Your opinion is important to us.

Discover more books by Mark Slade at
https://www.nextchapter.pub/authors/mark-slade

Want to know when one of our books is free or discounted? Join the newsletter at http://eepurl.com/bqqB3H

Best regards,
Mark Slade and the Next Chapter Team

You might also like:

Strange Corridors by Mark Slade

To read the first chapter for free, please head to:
https://www.nextchapter.pub/books/strange-corridors

About the Author

Mark Slade is the author of A Six Gun and the Queen of Light, Book of Weird, Blackout City Confidential, Mr Zero (Barry London series) Mean Business, and A Witch for Hire (Evelina Giles series) published by Horrified Press and Close to the Bone. He also writes, produces and directs the audio drama Blood Noir and writes the audio podcast drama Daniel Dread (with Lothar Tuppan, directed by Daniel French) and the weird western audio series The Sundowners. Currently (along with co-creator Lothar Tuppan) he is writing, producing, and Directing the radio show Twisted Pulp Radio hour for KKRN 88.5 in California.

He lives in Williamsburg, Va with his wife, daughter, and a Chihuahua that does funny impressions of famous actors.

Cameron Hampton is a Masters Circle Member of the International Association of Pastel Societies, earning her Gold Medal in the Spring of 2007. She is a painter, photographer, sculptor, cinematographer, animator and illustrator. Hampton attended both Pratt Institute in Brooklyn, New York and The Atlanta College of Art (now The Savannah College of Art and Design) in Atlanta, Georgia. Also, she has studied independently in Austria, Belgium, The Netherlands, Slovakia, England and Hungary, where she lived. Hampton has works in corporate and private collections throughout the world and has been represented by galleries in Amsterdam, The Netherlands, Atlanta, Georgia and Albuquerque, New Mexico, to name a few.

She now works and spends time in Georgia, USA., London, England and Utrecht, The Netherlands. Her work is currently represented by Carré d'Artistes in Mexico City, Mexico.

Yardbird
ISBN: 978-4-86750-881-7

Published by
Next Chapter
1-60-20 Minami-Otsuka
170-0005 Toshima-Ku, Tokyo
+818035793528
18th June 2021